BRUSSELS, DECEMBER 31, 1999

My name is Eva Stern. I was born with the century and, no doubt, will die with it. I knew Freud, met Stalin and Gandhi, heard Allen Ginsberg, Simone de Beauvoir, and the Rolling Stones, loved some, despised others, cried, hated, hoped, abandoned, betrayed. In short, I lived during the 20th Century... What else is there to say? At 98 years old, my words are becoming scarce and only a few images remain, usually without any captions...
As time goes by, everything goes away, Leo Ferré used to sing... As time goes by, it becomes impossible to judge, to justify, or simply to comment on my memories... Moreover, telling my story has never been my passion, I am a psychoanalyst and my life has always been listening to that of others...

YSLAIRE
From Cloud 99
http://www.xxeciel.com/memories part two

Humanoids Publishing™

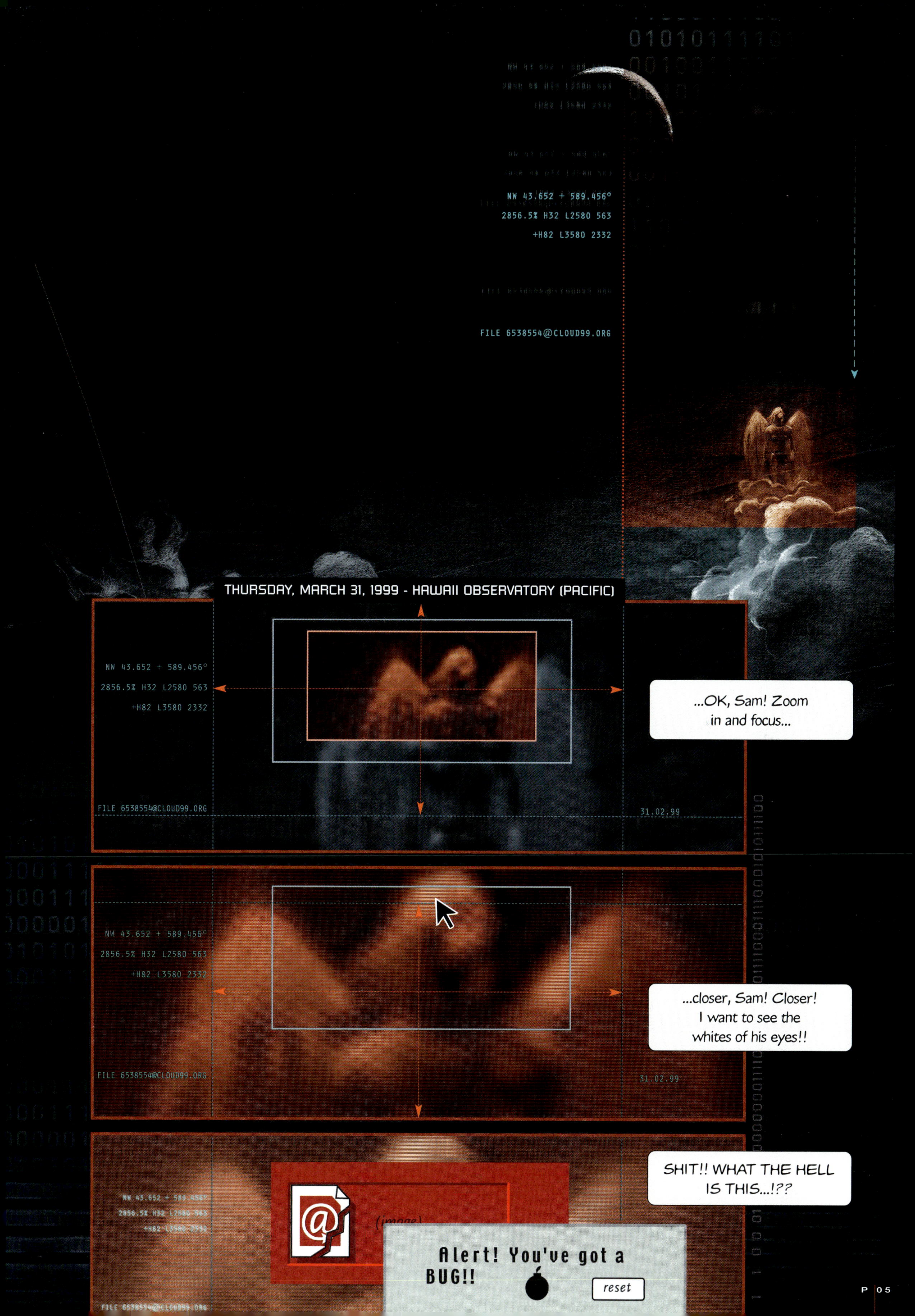

NW 43.652 + 589.456°
2856.5% H32 L2580 563
+H82 L3580 2332

FILE 6538554@CLOUD99.ORG

THURSDAY, MARCH 31, 1999 - HAWAII OBSERVATORY (PACIFIC)

NW 43.652 + 589.456°
2856.5% H32 L2580 563
+H82 L3580 2332
FILE 6538554@CLOUD99.ORG
31.02.99

...OK, Sam! Zoom in and focus...

NW 43.652 + 589.456°
2856.5% H32 L2580 563
+H82 L3580 2332
FILE 6538554@CLOUD99.ORG
31.02.99

...closer, Sam! Closer! I want to see the whites of his eyes!!

SHIT!! WHAT THE HELL IS THIS...!??

(image)

Alert! You've got a BUG!!

reset

...looks like there's a virus...

I betcha the generator's up to its usual tricks...
...hmm... it looks a lot like a virus... betcha 50 bucks that some geek hacked his way into the network...

You're joking, I hope? ...For thirty years I've been watching for an extraterrestrial to arrive from space and, when I finally pick one up, it's a hacker!?
Hey, Nate!? We both lost the bet! Come look!!

...longitude 246° 15' 25"... the computer has clearly picked up static from Vega... I'm requesting confirmation from Tucson, but that's not coming from any space station or satellite...

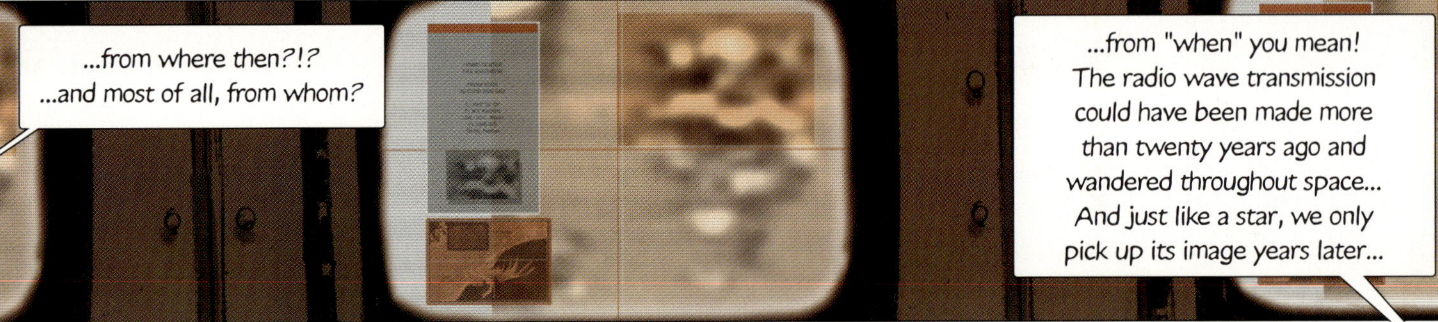
...from where then?!? ...and most of all, from whom?
...from "when" you mean! The radio wave transmission could have been made more than twenty years ago and wandered throughout space... And just like a star, we only pick up its image years later...

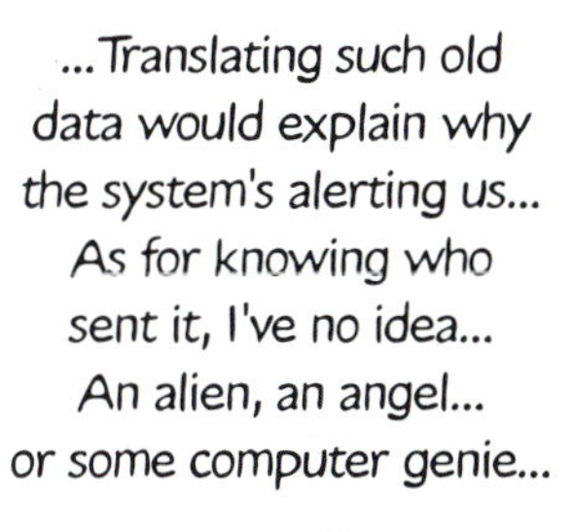

...Translating such old data would explain why the system's alerting us... As for knowing who sent it, I've no idea... An alien, an angel... or some computer genie...

...twenty years, you said... which takes us back to pre-Internet times... Yeah, it's possible...

...I was working for NASA back then... I may have already seen this picture...

...and have known the photographer as well as the astronaut photographed...

FILE 6538554@CLOUD99.ORG

It's even the last picture picked up by Houston during the Apollo 18 rescue... classified, obviously...

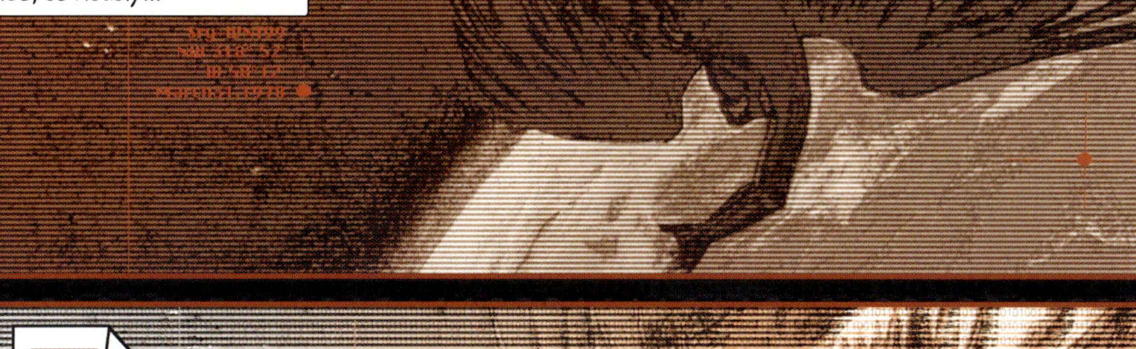

Alert! You've got a BUG!!
reset
SHIT!! It's happening again...

@

Tuscon confirms, Nate. It's not coming from one of our satellites nor the Russkies'... God knows who's trying to send us a message... But he'll remain anonymous!... New image, Nate...

April 1st 1999 e-mail from Nathan Uriel to Raphaël <wergifüss@nasa.org

Hawaii Observatory. Report of April 1, 1999 to Raphael Von Wergifüss<wergifüss@nasa.org

Hey, Raph! Tell me I'm dreaming! This morning, the Observatory's central computer recorded some close-range static. The image-conversion of the data clearly showed a satellite photo of an angel walking on clouds in the stratosphere.

At first, since it's April 1st, I thought it was a gag sent by some old, nostalgic astrophysicist, crazy enough to be sending photos from his younger days by satellite link... until the central computer confirmed the presence of an "alien" in the scan zone. Right when I zoomed in to locate it, I got a virus alert... Tell me, doesn't that remind you of Gabe's song "Angel Walking on Cloud 99"? ...and the Apollo 18 mission? ...By the way, any news about Frank Stern? Do you reckon he's dead? Nate.

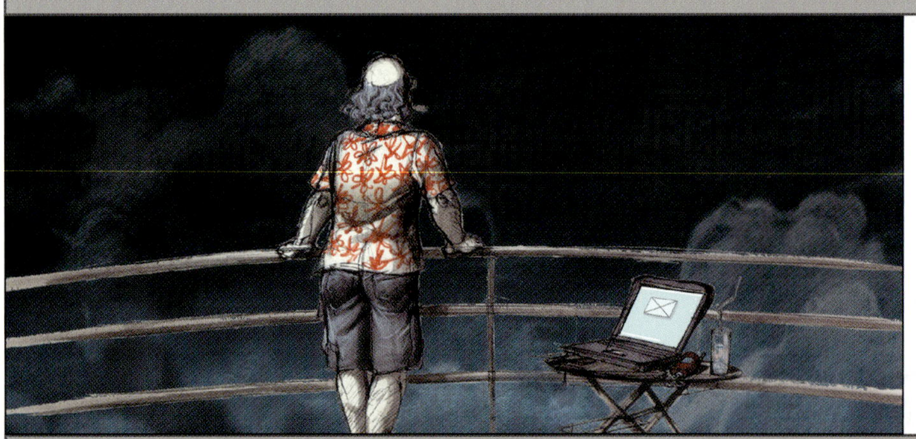

April 2nd 1999 From Raphaël von Wergifüss to nathan.uriel@xxciel.com

Orlando, April 2, 1999. Sorry, Nate. I'm on vacation and I don't know what you're talking about. Moreover, Apollo 18 is a mission that never took place. To answer you about Frank, there's only his sister Eva Stern. If she's still alive...
Keep in touch. <wergifüss@nasa.org

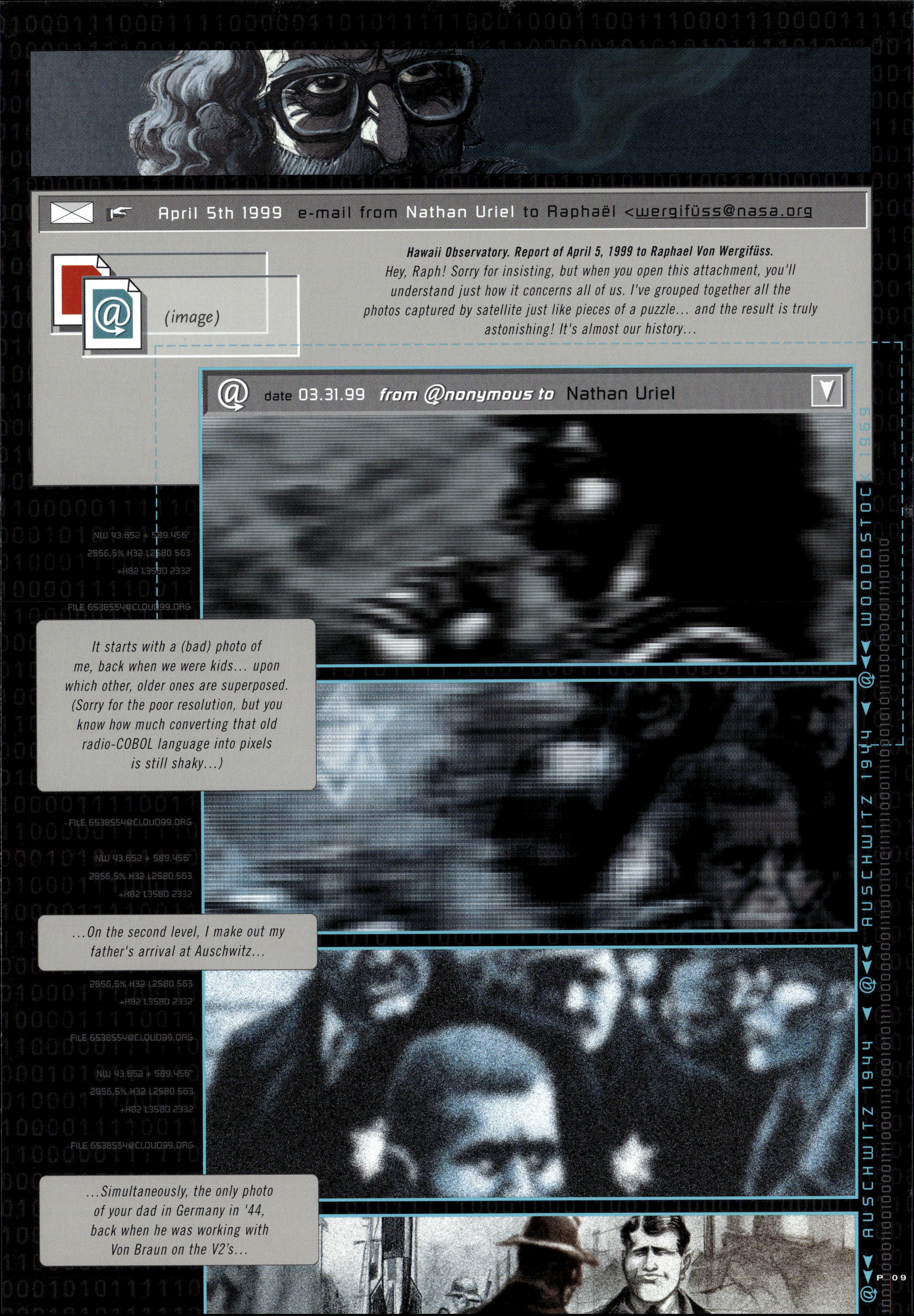

April 5th 1999 e-mail from Nathan Uriel to Raphaël <wergifüss@nasa.org>

(image)

Hawaii Observatory. Report of April 5, 1999 to Raphael Von Wergifüss.

Hey, Raph! Sorry for insisting, but when you open this attachment, you'll understand just how it concerns all of us. I've grouped together all the photos captured by satellite just like pieces of a puzzle... and the result is truly astonishing! It's almost our history...

date 03.31.99 **from @nonymous to** Nathan Uriel

It starts with a (bad) photo of me, back when we were kids... upon which other, older ones are superposed. (Sorry for the poor resolution, but you know how much converting that old radio-COBOL language into pixels is still shaky...)

...On the second level, I make out my father's arrival at Auschwitz...

...Simultaneously, the only photo of your dad in Germany in '44, back when he was working with Von Braun on the V2's...

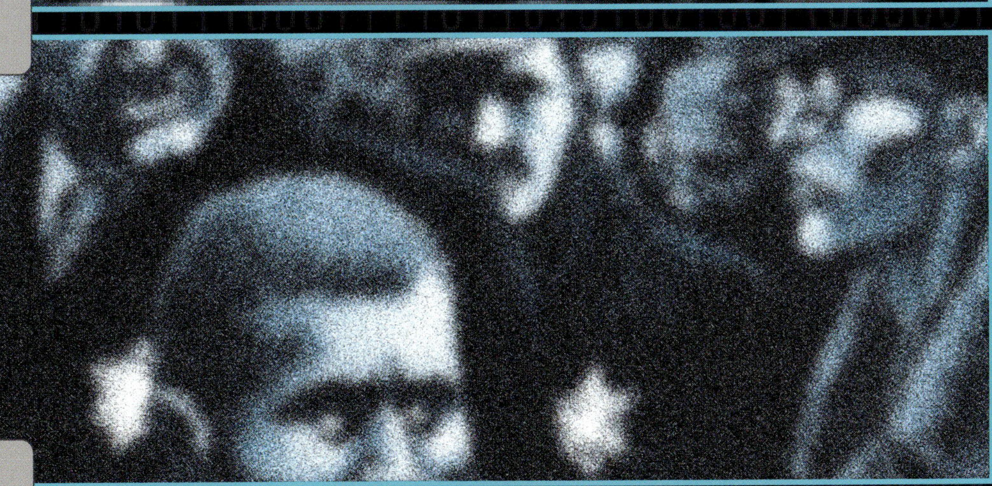

WOODSTOCK 1969 — AUSCHWITZ 1944 — AUSCHWITZ 1944

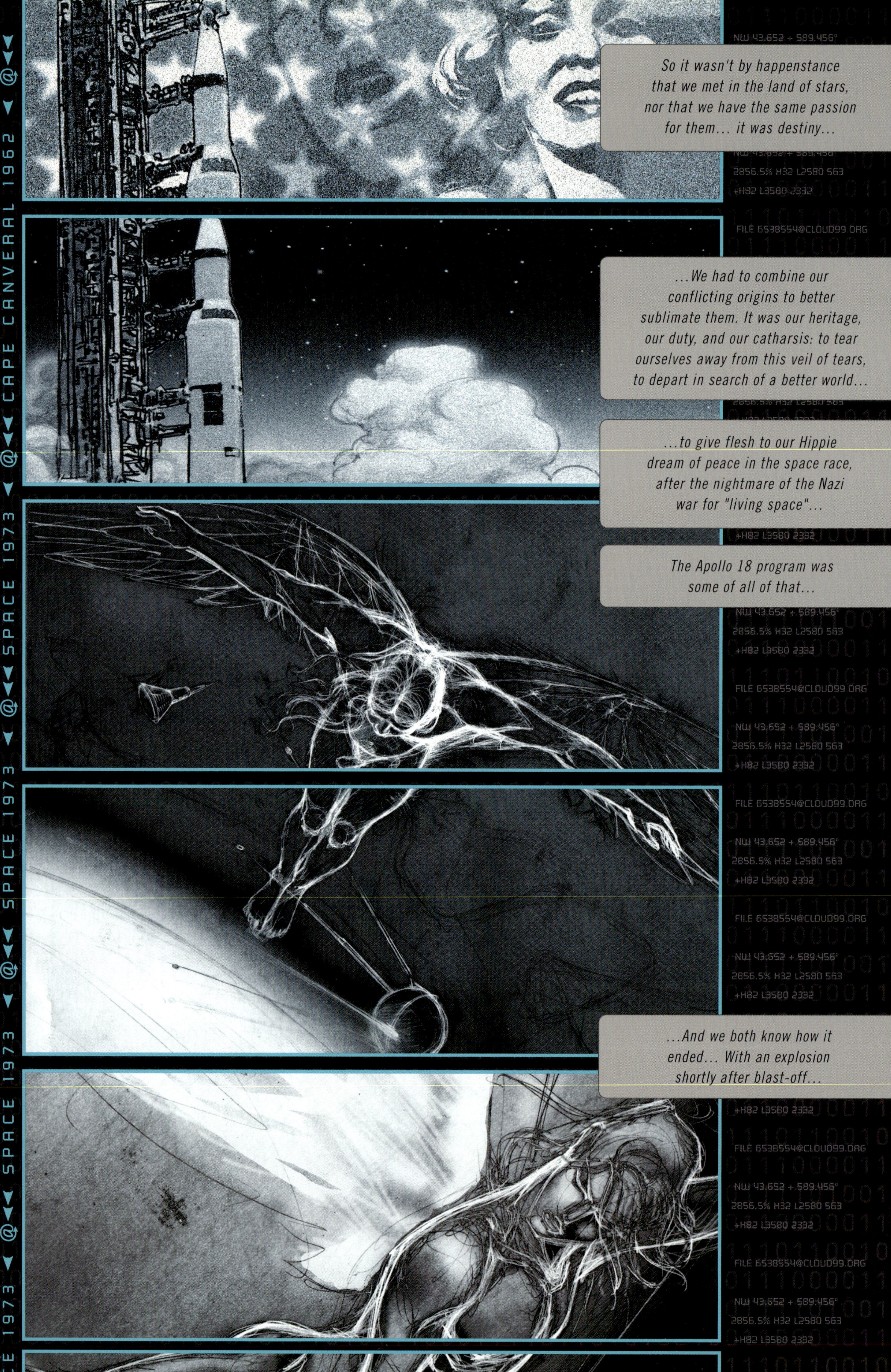

So it wasn't by happenstance that we met in the land of stars, nor that we have the same passion for them... it was destiny...
...We had to combine our conflicting origins to better sublimate them. It was our heritage, our duty, and our catharsis: to tear ourselves away from this veil of tears, to depart in search of a better world...
...to give flesh to our Hippie dream of peace in the space race, after the nightmare of the Nazi war for "living space"...
The Apollo 18 program was some of all of that...
...And we both know how it ended... With an explosion shortly after blast-off...

...But tell me, my friend... You, the astronaut hidden behind Skylab's porthole, the one who commanded the Apollo 18 rescue mission... did you see an angel flying amidst the debris?
...And if that's not the case, put me at ease: didn't Frank Stern take these shots?...
Alert! You've got a BUG!!
reset
SPACE 1973 @ e-mail from @nonymous
April 5th 1999 From Raphaël von Wergifüss to nathan.uriel@xxciel.com

Orlando, April 5, 1999

Dear Nathan. As usual, you're mistaking your desire for extraterrestrials for reality. As for the photos, let me remind you that the first Apollo missions abandoned all their photo materials on the moon to lighten themsel es as much as possible. Nobody knows exactly what got filmed... because no one went back for it! Saying that those images come from the aforementioned film comes under the heading of a hoax or manipulating history... Which ine itably brings us back to that de il Frank Stern. Now you know as well as I that it's impossible for him to ha e participated or sur i ed that trip. The last person to ha e crossed paths with him was Gabriel Da ies in 1971 and it was in a hospital. Knowing the ambitions of our surgeon friend, and knowing what happened in Brussels in '71, we could probably suppose that he donated the Austrian's body to science... <wergifüss@nasa.org>

MAY 14, 1999 - ORLANDO [FLORIDA]

...in weather like this, Raph's in the shade surfing the Web...
Hmm...

Tell me why astronauts hate the sun so much?
Because it's got a temperature of 5000°Celsius there and you have to be like Icarus to get close to it. I'm more down to earth, you know...

So I see. Very down to earth! ...but pretty hot, too...

You'll be surprised, Honey, but I'm not visiting a porn site. I'm reading an e-mail.

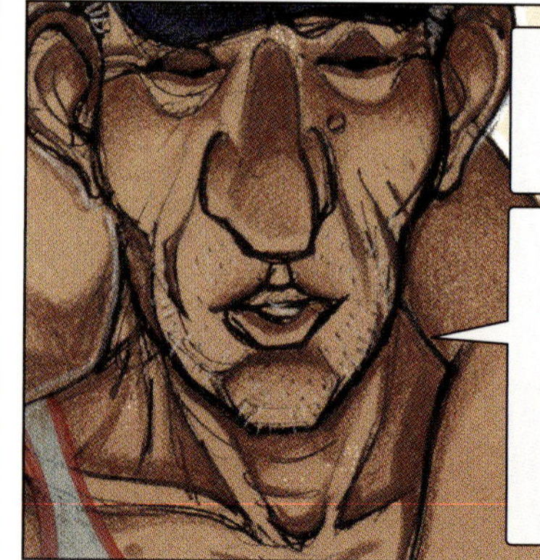

You call that reading? You're getting an eyeful!
You don't understand. Someone is sending me images via e-mail... with no word of explanation... Someone who knows me well...

You might say so! You've always got one thing on your mind...
Look at all of them before you judge...
date 04.31.99 from @nonymous to Raphaël von Wergifüss
That's a picture of me during the 60's... Strange, isn't it?
Have I told you before that the Apollo II ship that landed on the moon was called the "Eagle"?
I don't see the connection...
Look... the Nazi eagle and the dove of peace...When you realize that my father was in the Nazi party during the war, and that I'm an astronaut and a pacifist...
...It's like a rebus...
K 1969 @ MOON 1972 @ PEENEMUNDE 1945 @ WOODSTOCK 1969
31.04.99 e-mail from @nonymous to Raphaël von Wergifüss
P 01

Wait, you'll get it.
From here on, it gets
more concrete...

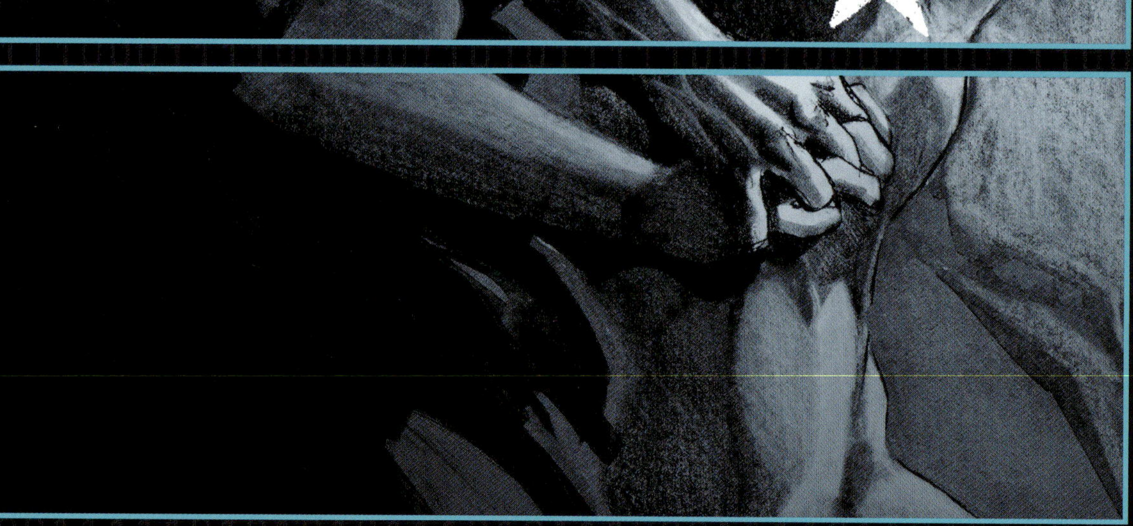

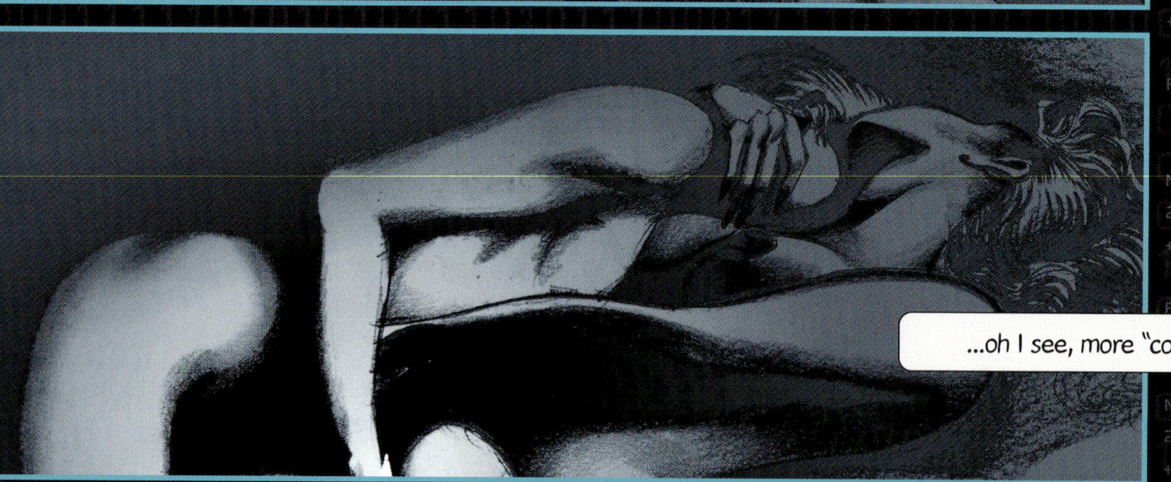

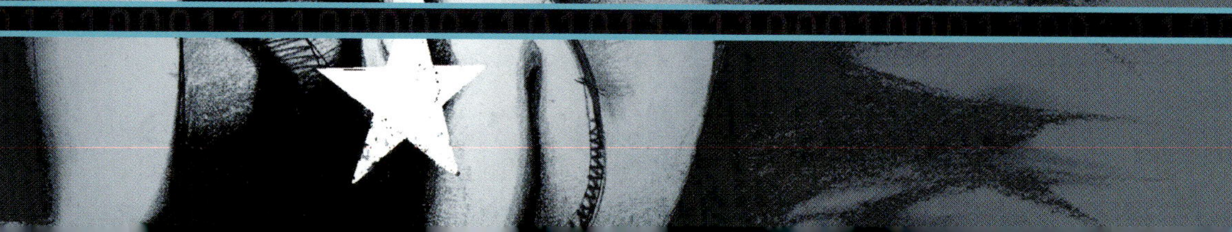

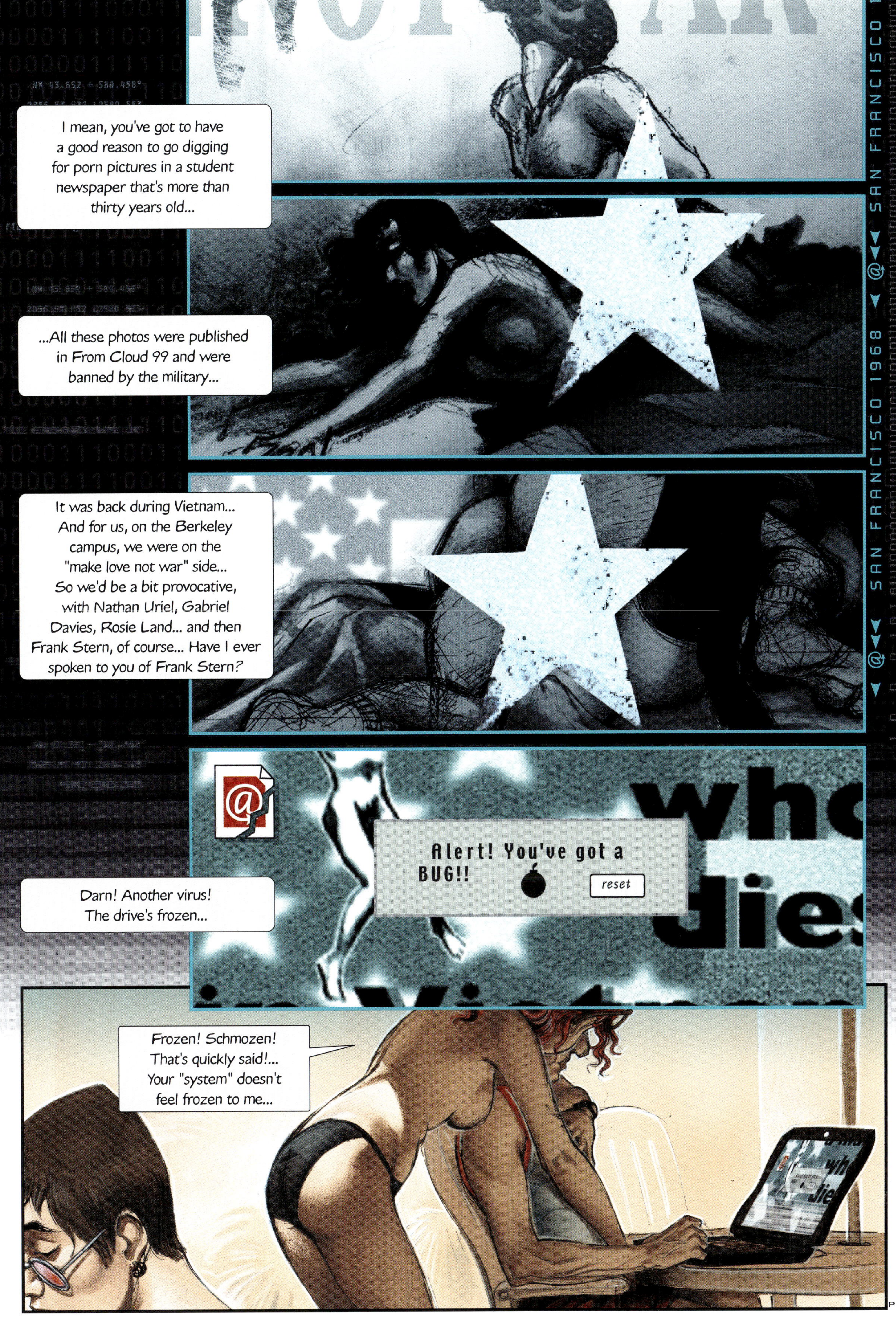
I mean, you've got to have a good reason to go digging for porn pictures in a student newspaper that's more than thirty years old...
...All these photos were published in From Cloud 99 and were banned by the military...
It was back during Vietnam... And for us, on the Berkeley campus, we were on the "make love not war" side... So we'd be a bit provocative, with Nathan Uriel, Gabriel Davies, Rosie Land... and then Frank Stern, of course... Have I ever spoken to you of Frank Stern?
Alert! You've got a BUG!!
reset
Darn! Another virus! The drive's frozen...
Frozen! Schmozen! That's quickly said!... Your "system" doesn't feel frozen to me...
SAN FRANCISCO 1968
SAN FRANCISCO 1968

This is a man who dies

CLOUD 9
NEWS FROM THE ANGELS APRIL 67
...NOT WAR!

Now I know why you'll never have any kids, Raphael... Because, like all astronauts, you've got stars on your mind... and, like stars, you're living in the past...
a Star
This is a man who dies Vietnam

Michael died in Vietnam, Gabriel has exiled himself to the chic hospitals of London, and Nathan is ending his career in Hawaii. As for Frank Stern, nobody knows where he is anymore...THE ARCHANGELS HAVE PASSED ON, Raphael!!!

Who knows, Shirley? Remembering is a kind of surviving, isn't it? And apparently, a certain @nonymous remembers archangels...

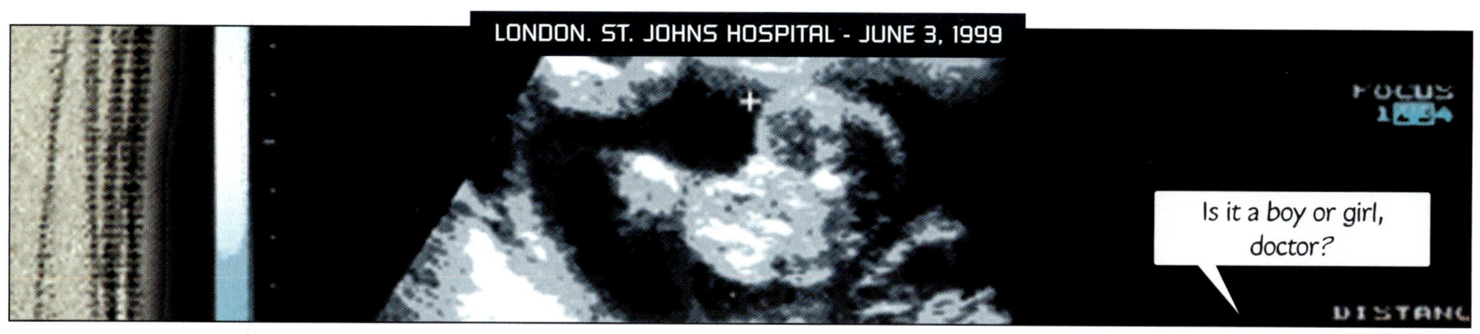
LONDON. ST. JOHNS HOSPITAL - JUNE 3, 1999
Is it a boy or girl, doctor?

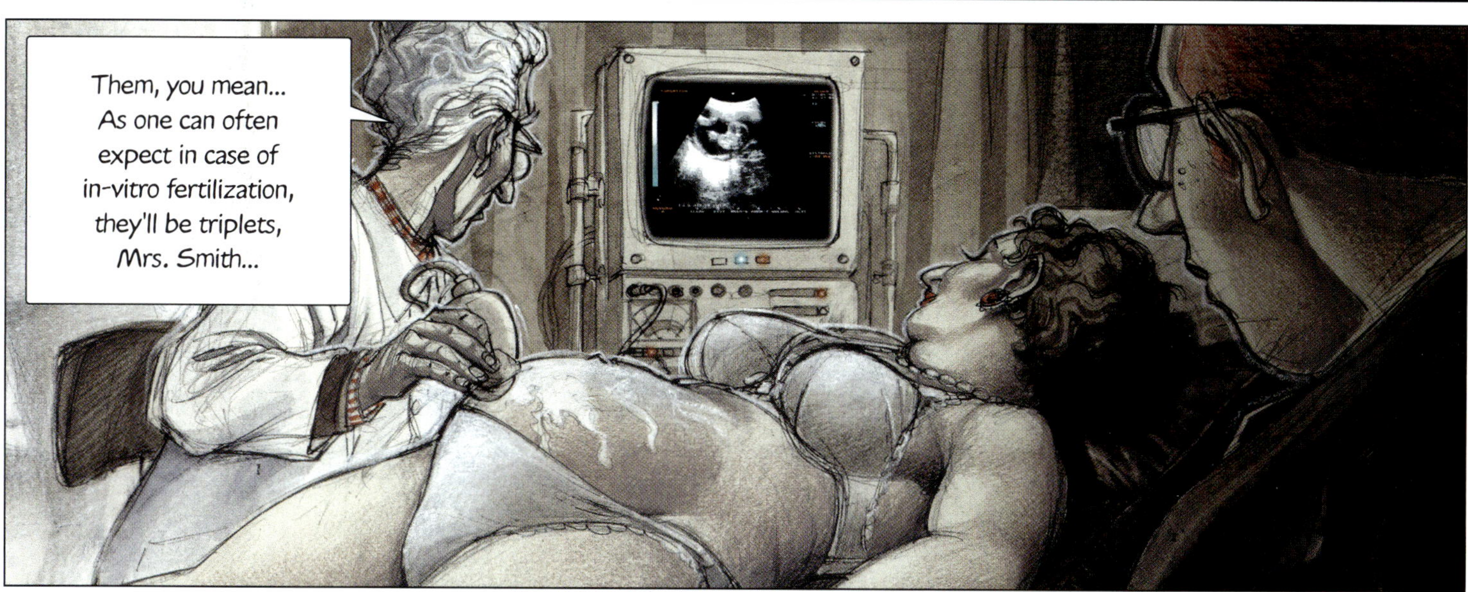
Them, you mean... As one can often expect in case of in-vitro fertilization, they'll be triplets, Mrs. Smith...

...I see a fine cowboy, a future mother and... and... I'm having trouble making out the third one's identity...

Hey! What's wrong, doctor?

Nothing more than a breakdown in the computer network, Mrs. Smith. A virus, as they say... it's only temporary...

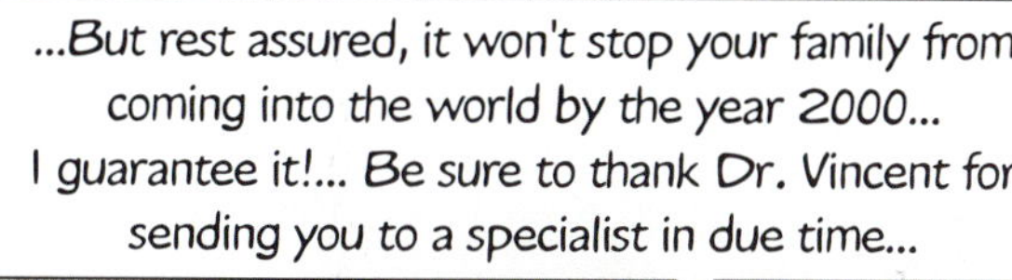
...But rest assured, it won't stop your family from coming into the world by the year 2000... I guarantee it!... Be sure to thank Dr. Vincent for sending you to a specialist in due time...

Oh well! Looks to me like it's fixed...

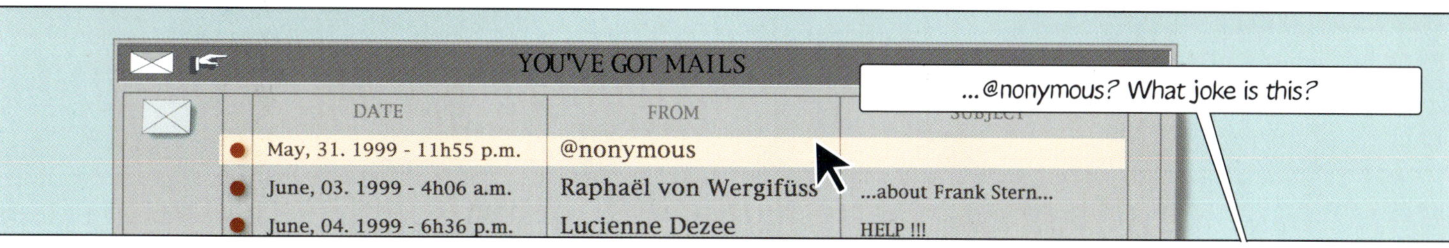
YOU'VE GOT MAILS
DATE
FROM
May, 31. 1999 - 11h55 p.m.
@nonymous
June, 03. 1999 - 4h06 a.m.
Raphaël von Wergifüss
...about Frank Stern...
June, 04. 1999 - 6h36 p.m.
Lucienne Dezee
HELP !!!
...@nonymous? What joke is this?

@ date 05.31.99 *from @nonymous to* Gabriel Davies

NW 43.652 + 589.456°
2856.5% H32 L2580 563
+H82 L3580 2332

FILE 6538554@CLOUD99.ORG

NW 43.652 + 589.456°
2856.5% H32 L2580 563
+H82 L3580 2332

FILE 6538554@CLOUD99.ORG

MOON 1973 @ STOCKOLM 1964 e-mail from @nonymous to Gabriel davies 31.05.99 MOON 1973 @ MOON 1973 @ MOON 1973

NW 43.652 + 589.456°
2856.5% H32 L2580 563
+H82 L3580 2332

FILE 6538554@CLOUD99.ORG

NW 43.652 + 589.456°
2856.5% H32 L2580 563
+H82 L3580 2332

FILE 6538554@CLOUD99.ORG

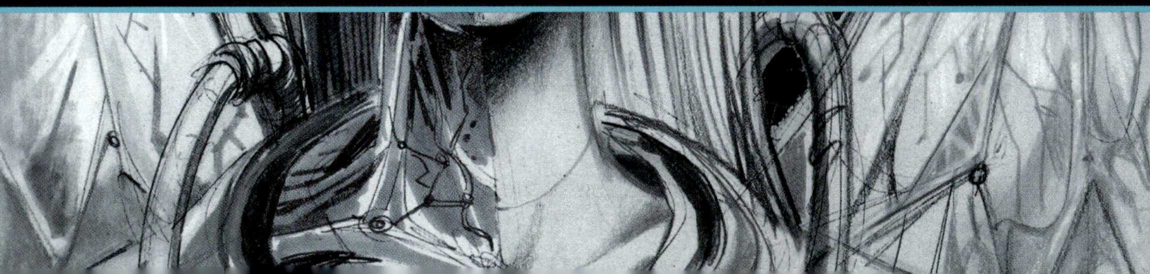

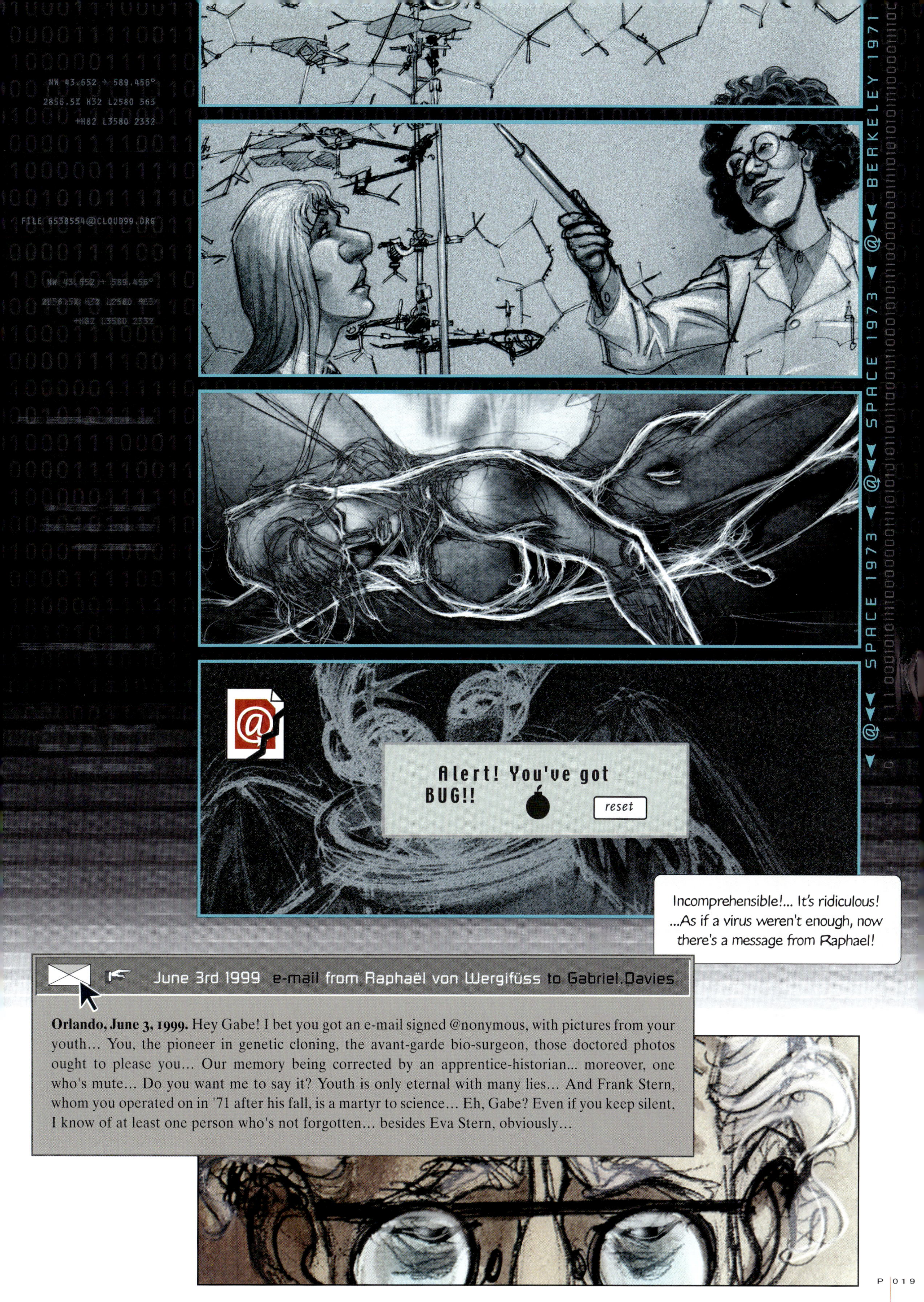

Alert! You've got BUG!!

reset

Incomprehensible!... It's ridiculous! ...As if a virus weren't enough, now there's a message from Raphael!

June 3rd 1999 e-mail from Raphaël von Wergifüss to Gabriel.Davies

Orlando, June 3, 1999. Hey Gabe! I bet you got an e-mail signed @nonymous, with pictures from your youth… You, the pioneer in genetic cloning, the avant-garde bio-surgeon, those doctored photos ought to please you… Our memory being corrected by an apprentice-historian… moreover, one who's mute… Do you want me to say it? Youth is only eternal with many lies… And Frank Stern, whom you operated on in '71 after his fall, is a martyr to science… Eh, Gabe? Even if you keep silent, I know of at least one person who's not forgotten… besides Eva Stern, obviously…

BRUSSELS, JUNE 31, 1999

DRRRR...
DRRRR...
...clac !!
BEEP! ...This is Eva Stern's answering machine. Please leave a message after the beep... BEEP!

...Hello, Eva. It's me Nathan Uriel again. Do you remember me?...I've been trying desperately to reach you for several weeks. I hope everything's going well with you health-wise...

...Please, call me back as soon as possible, it's important... I think I have news about Frank...

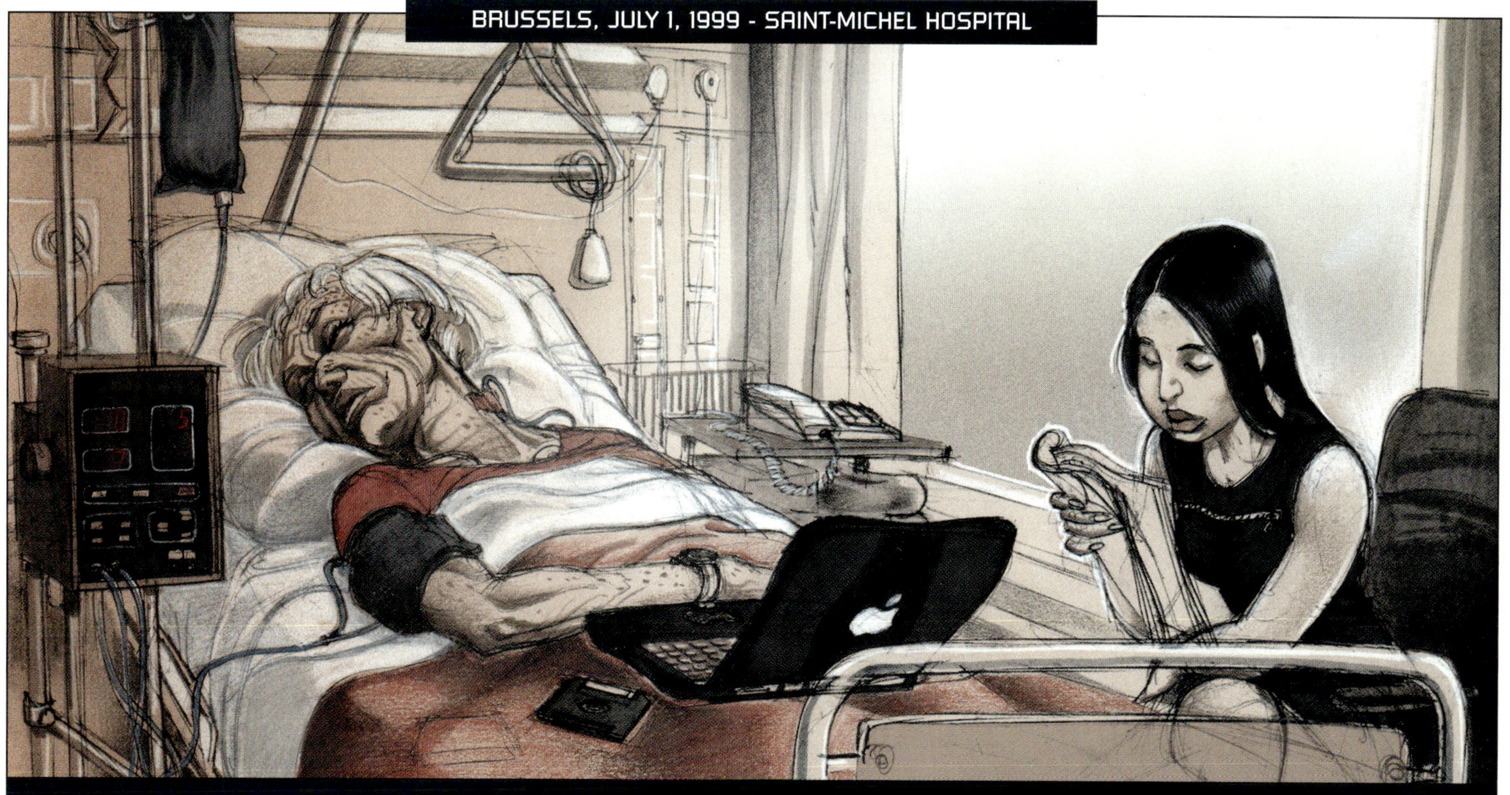

I'm not dead yet. A nasty brain tumor has kept me bedridden for months and keeps me silent. The nights are especially painful, but I'm not complaining. Living for 99 years is already pretty good. Ever since they admitted me to Intensive Care, a day doesn't go by without Lucienne coming to see me. For obscure reasons, she's gotten attached to this 99 year-old nanny goat. I don't know if she'll ever finish that paper on the history of psychoanalysis... or if I'll be able to help her very much...

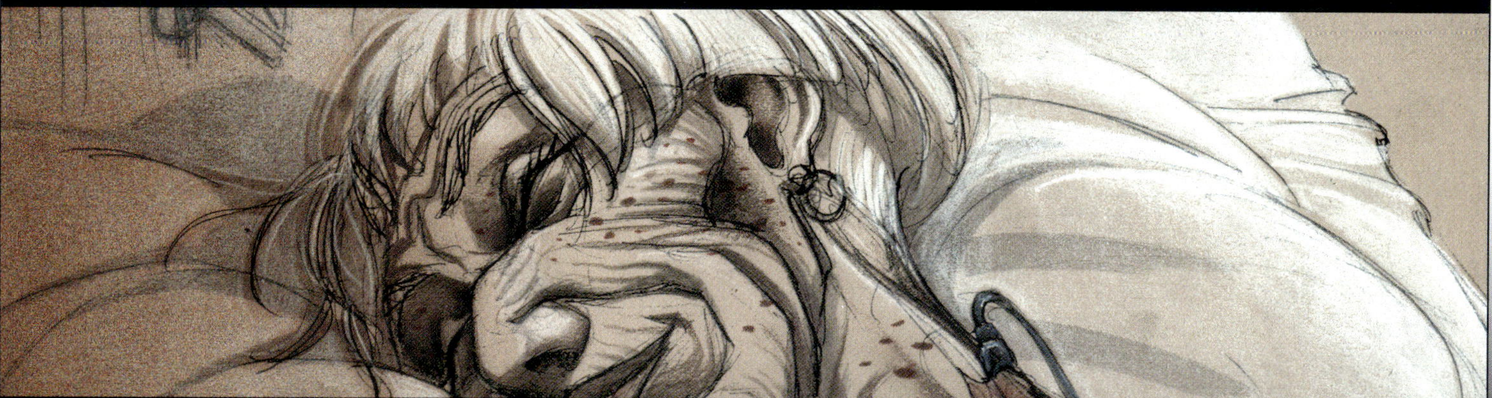

Meanwhile, the youngster brings me my mail daily, both written and electronic. This Tuesday, I got another e-mail from @noymous.

date 06.31.99 **from @nonymous to** Eva Stern <evastern@yslaire.be

(image)

Even if he went silent for these very long months, @nonymous isn't forgetting me. @noymous loves me. @nonymous is an angel... lost on the Moon, who remembers my century...

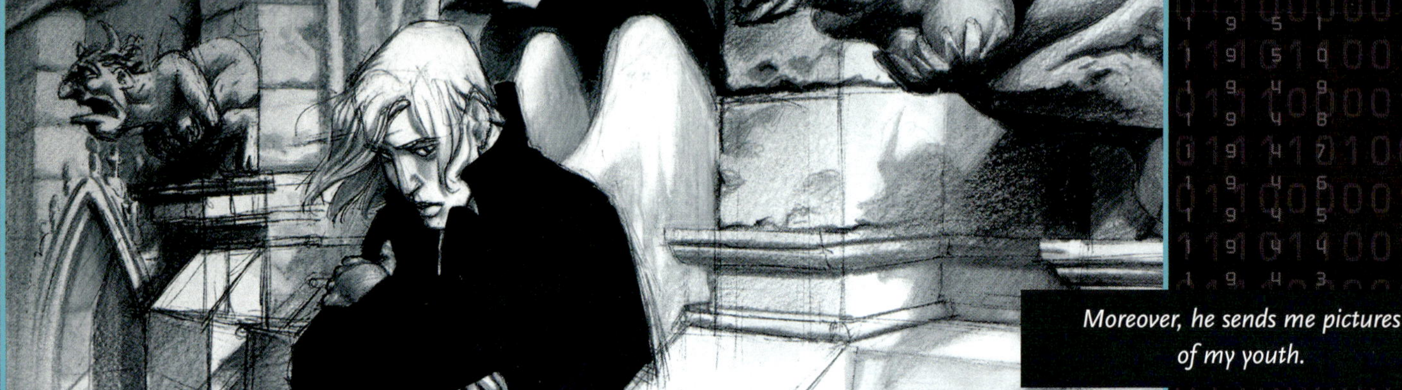
Moreover, he sends me pictures of my youth.

Thanks to him, I'm still alive. I'm reliving that winter of 1916...

...I'm reborn...

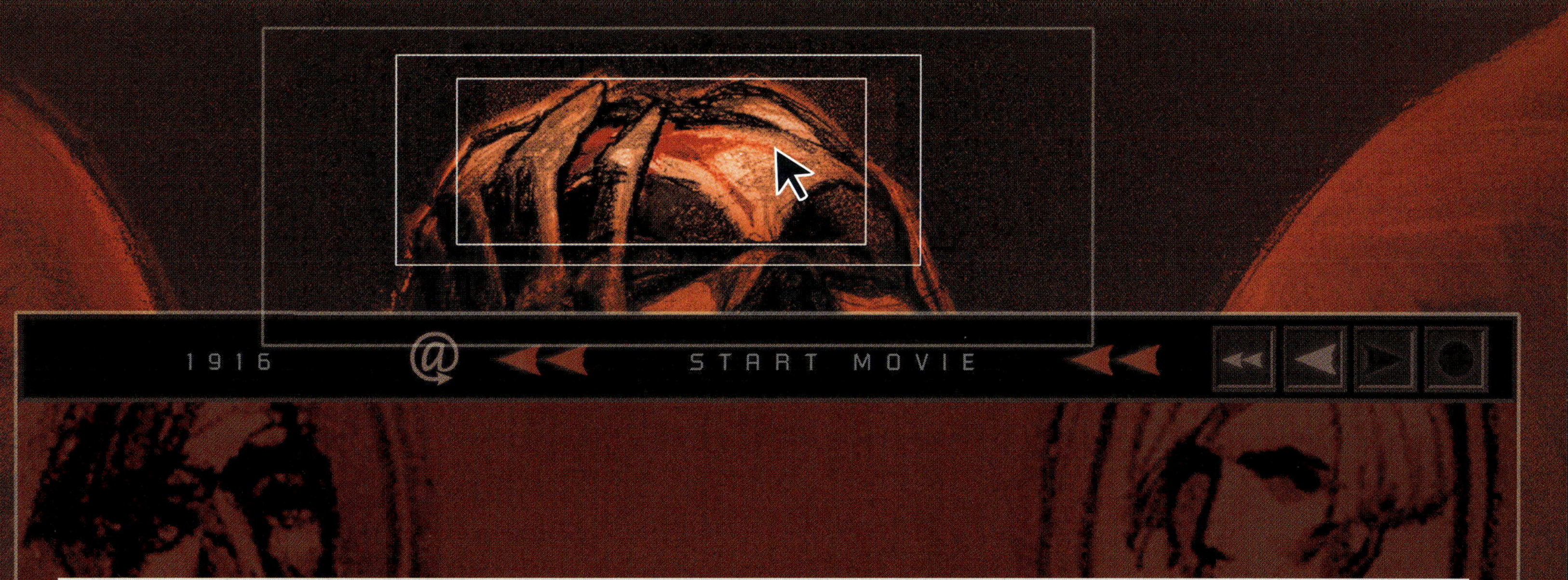

1916 @ START MOVIE

@ VIENNA, OCT. 22, 1916

AUGUST STERN
(1842-1906)
FRANK E. STERN

Click. Start Movie... I'm reliving that 22nd of October 1916. The weather is rather glacial. All of Vienna is pressing at the gates of the Schönrunn. The father of the nation, Emperor Franz-Josef has succumbed to pneumonia. The same day, many fewer people are at the Kahlenberg cemetery for the burial of Frank Stern, fallen in combat. My mother, the concierge and her son, a comrade from the trenches, and myself. Everyone weeps over that interminable war. Mama despairs that it has carried off her "little angel"...

I cannot console her. I know that the body they've buried has a shattered head, which makes him an unknown soldier. But I cannot make her party to my doubts as to his identity... No more than I could confide in her my hopes that he had deserted to Switzerland.

...And that old man observing me from afar only added to my unease...

At the cemetery's exit, he hands me the second issue of that banned newspaper. I insult him for the grotesquerie of his action in such circumstances... He gives me a threatening look and heads away. Luckily, mama didn't see anything...

Rédacteur

Directeur:Fabienne Rougedyeu

LE XXe CIEL

JOURNAL DES AMES — 31 NOVEMBRE 1916 — 1e Année -N° 3

Ich bin ewig!

(Je suis éternel!)

...Over the following weeks, I conceal the newspaper from her and keep its contents quiet. Frank deserting to Switzerland, Frank in the arms of a Frenchwoman, Frank in Zurich in the company of one Vladimir Oulianov and the first Bolsheviks... To sum up in one word, as in one hundred photos, her dear son, if living, was betraying her as much as the homeland. It's too much provocation, too much emotion for her... Ich bin ewig, I am eternal, the headline reads, but who is, in this year of 1916?

On December 30th, mama doesn't wake up...

Did she search my room? Did I hide it poorly? ...I find her in the morning, her head hidden under the pages of the paper. She leaves me while holding the crumpled paper over her chest. And she's smiling... For the first time in an eternity.

Four days later, my mind's made up. While returning from the Zentralfriedhof, I voluntarily wander towards the Judenplatz. Here, most of the disabled soldiers, kept from public view, are to be found on the same sidewalks as the Jewish tailors. I quickly locate the neighborhood's disabled soldiers' center.

At the entrance, I ask a young soldier if he knows of the XXe Ciel. He answers by asking me for the time, today's date, and his name. He repeats himself and insists with a sleight grin. Obviously, combat stress has affected his brain.

I go into the shop of a bird-catcher that had gone to the front. All his cages are empty. Despite the noise from the street, I heard a crow's cawing...

The one-armed man doesn't seem surprised to see me. Or he's drunk. I repeat my question to him. He stares at me and looks me up and down. I'm uncomfortable.

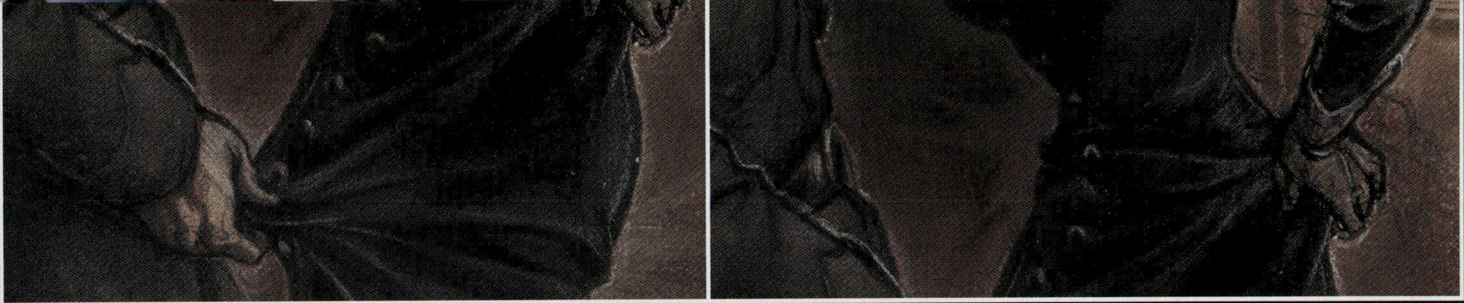

His hand catches the bottom of my skirt and tries to lift it. I defend myself as best I can. "What do you want?" he growls.

I tell him about the XXe Ciel, that I'm looking for its editor, that I understand his suffering, that I'd like for him to help me get into Switzerland, to find my brother again... I blush, I mumble, and I stay there, as paralyzed as his arm... "Everyone wants help here," he mutters.

He finally lets go of my skirt. I hear noises in the shadows and I understand why the cages are empty... And I see them pressing about, devouring me with their eyes. "Don't worry, they're no longer dangerous... " he says, giving way to them. They thought they were giving their lives for their country, but they've only lost their minds. They no longer even know their mothers' names...

It's more than I can take. I want to help them. So, I remind them where they come from...

I understood that day everything that separates me from my brother. My angels are innocent, devoid of guilt because they're crazy. The crazy messengers of a mute god. I spend my life trying to make them speak... I will spend my life trying to rejoin him...

I wasn't mistaken. Like many of the veterans, the crow-man is a member of the Austrian branch of the Bolshevik movement. He even met Frank at Isonzo. It's in that spirit of propaganda that he's slyly handing out the XXe Ciel to a public opposing the imperial regime, the "defeatists" as the official press calls them. After some necessary precautions and a "spontaneous" contribution to the Party's coffers, and with a smuggler's help, I secretly cross into Switzerland. I arrive at Sion on March 14, 1917. Werner Ysler welcomes me. I have a rendezvous at the Hotel de la Poste with Fabienne Rouge-Dyeu. She's to lead me to Frank.

She welcomes me warmly. Werner Ysler is at her side. Both are kind, polite. When I ask them where Frank is, they look at one another with a hint of connivance. "In Zurich," she answers. "Haven't you seen the news?"

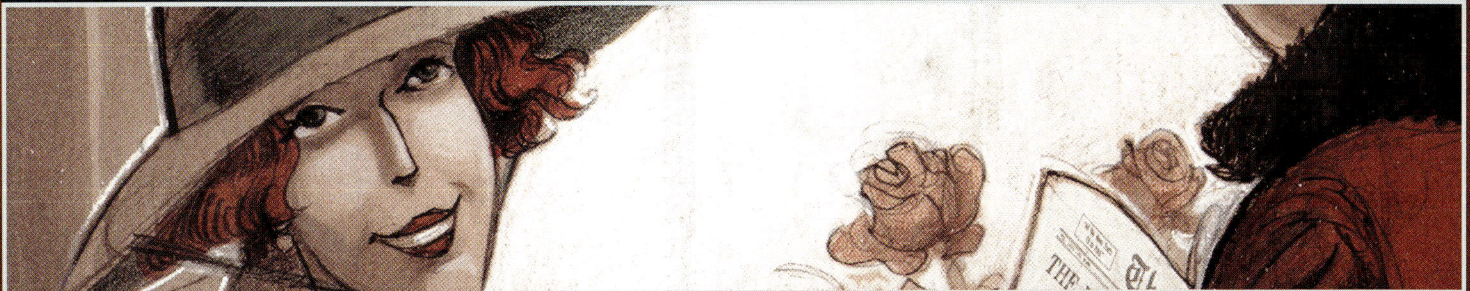

She proudly hands me a copy of the Times. The czar has abdicated; the revolution is underway. She unofficially announces to me the Bolshevik leader's intentions who, exiled to Switzerland, will return to Russia (with the assistance of the German military)... and, according to her, to carry the good news (to put an end to the war on the Eastern Front, according to German desires)...Frank, the official photographer, will follow along. She herself will rejoin them later, in a week, with the second train of revolutionaries.

I can understand your disappointment, but just think, it's a world-scale event, an exceptional opportunity. We're going to be able to change the world! she blazes. That's why it's essential for Frank to follow Lenin to Petrograd. So the world can see and know that the XXe Ciel really does exist and that it's being born in Russia right now!

Times.

MANOFF DYNASTY
ENDED IN RUSSIA

Violents
French
RESISTS

She's convinced. She also tells me of their passionate meetings with the Bolshevik leader and Frank's enthusiasm about the idea of a more just society, which would create a model for the new man...

The young Austrian believes in bettering human beings, in the possibility of a spiritual elevation "resulting from History." And combining gestures with words, he lifts his arms to the sky. As if to fly away...

A more down-to-earth Lenin distrusts angels as much as the XXè Ciel. At most, he puts up with the paper's success for the sake of the revolutionary fervor it provokes. Moreover, he never lifts but one arm. To salute his Party comrades or to quiet the assembly. "As if to reach for our star," he says ironically. "With a sickle in hand, if necessary." Hearing him, I already understand that that star will be covered in blood... And before others raise their arms in the same fashion and attempt to extinguish every star...

And she laughs. As happy and unconscious as a teenager before the first time they run away. She's only eighteen...I observe her and remain silent.

I know that I won't go to Russia and that I won't see Frank again.

We share a little more small talk, but all of Fabienne Rouge Dyeu's cheerfulness doesn't succeed in masking the unease arising between us. I read in her eyes that she's hiding something from me...

...And I feel "his" presence nearby... Behind the wall hangings...

Once I arrive back to my room, I'm slow to fall asleep. I've crossed Austria and the Jura Mountains to see my brother alive. I now guess that it's no longer death that separates us. It's a utopia...

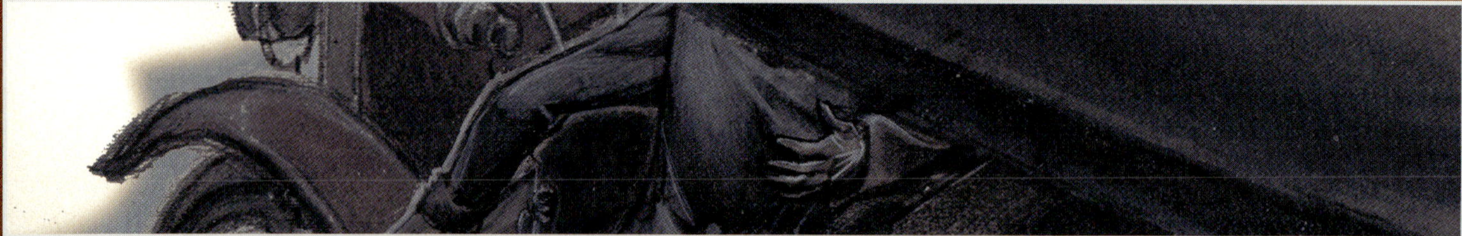
...Yes, the young Frenchwoman has lied to me. Frank isn't inZurich yet. He's hiding, not far from here. And she joins him every night.

I get my confirmation at breakfast, between the coffeepot and the morning paper.

...Someone has left an anonymous envelope.
With photos, without a word.

1999/@ - SION/1917 ....0011110101:31:02:99

...And its message is clear...

1999/@ - SION/1917 ....0011110101:31:02:99

...After his fashion, "He" tells me what Fabienne Rouge-Dyeu had so sought to conceal from me... Frank loves the Frenchwoman, and the Frenchwoman loves Frank. It's a matter of flesh...

...In other words, HE is there, very alive, in all the shots... HE observes us and photographs himself...
My brother, my witness, my soul mate...

...And I would never see HIM again...HE would always be invisible to me...
unless it were in photos...

SION 1917 © 1999

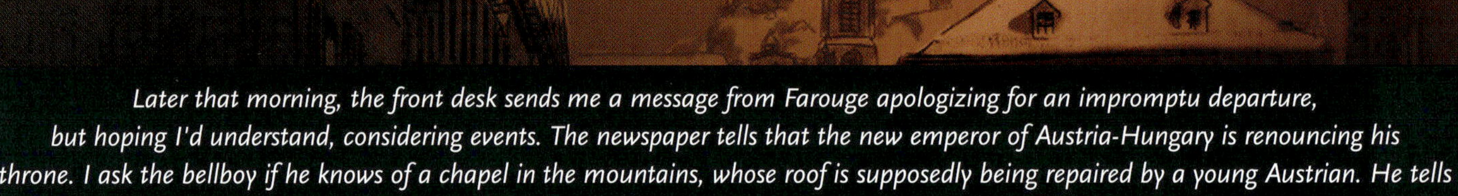

Later that morning, the front desk sends me a message from Farouge apologizing for an impromptu departure, but hoping I'd understand, considering events. The newspaper tells that the new emperor of Austria-Hungary is renouncing his throne. I ask the bellboy if he knows of a chapel in the mountains, whose roof is supposedly being repaired by a young Austrian. He tells me that he can think of only one fitting my description, and shows me the way to get there.

En route, I cross a multitude of tracks in the snow going the other way... The departure must have been hasty.
Indeed, the chapel's door was left open.

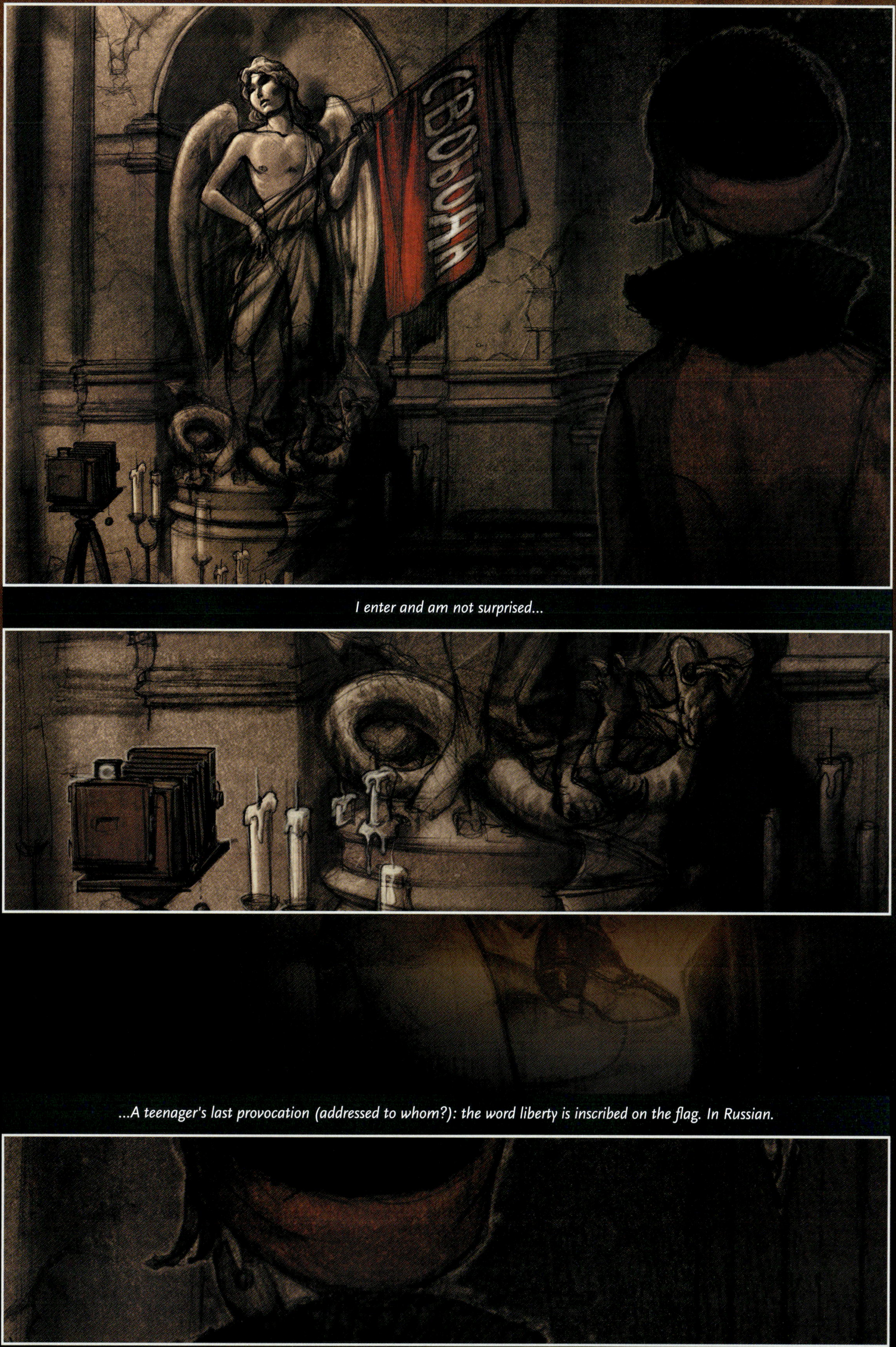

I enter and am not surprised...

...A teenager's last provocation (addressed to whom?): the word liberty is inscribed on the flag. In Russian.

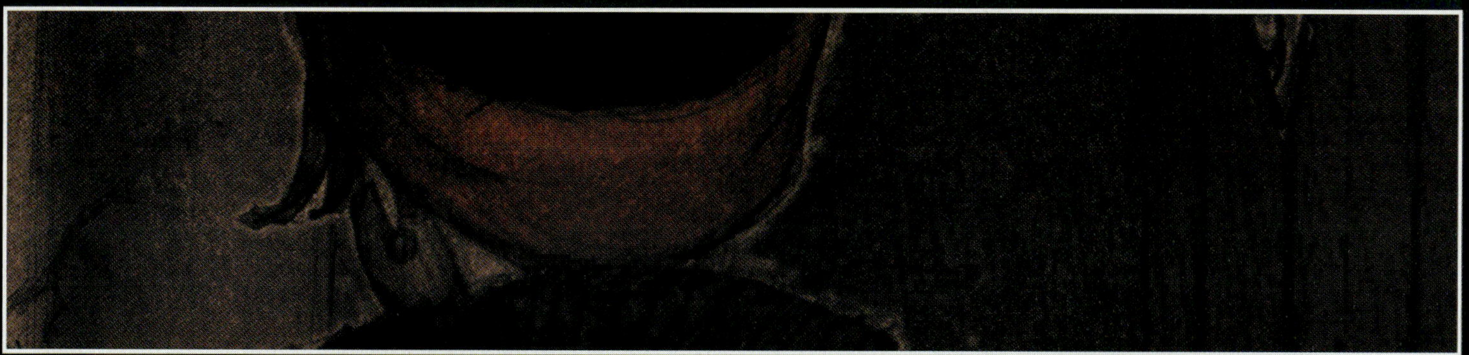

March 31, 1917. Click. Return to Vienna. A smell of defeat hangs in the air. The ninth offensive upon Isonzo ended in bitter failure for the two armies. As did the previous ones...

I resume my habits, my work as a nurse, my sessions with Freud. But my mind is elsewhere...

...It's still in Switzerland, in a chapel near Sion...

April, 1917. With Freud's recommendation, I'm beginning a psychiatric internship at Steinhof. At this time, for lack of space, the Viennese asylum houses psychotics, neurotics, and battle-fatigue victims all in the same rooms. Upon my arrival, I cannot avoid crossing the gaze of the sculpted angels of Otto Wagner: their compassion seems eternal...

The months pass. I follow events in the international press with a slight delay. Via published photos, I reconstruct my brother's epic in Russia. His departure in an armored train from Zurich on March 17th, his arrival in Moscow, his passionate liaison with Farouge...

At this time, Frank is in the shadow of the Bolshevik ringleader... and the XXe Ciel that appears on November 17th hides neither his devotion nor his blindness for the cause. He serves the Party's propaganda.

31 Octobre 1917
OKTЯБРЬ
Ils ont accroché une étoile au dessus du Palais d'Hiver
Petrograd 28 octobre. Devant le palais d'Hiver … foule des révolutionnaires et sympathisants bolchéviques attend. Parmi eux, se m… des personnalités en vue dont le journaliste américain John Reed et l'aviatrice … aise, Fabienne Rouge-Dy… Tous deux, et quelques autres moins connus, ont suivi … leur dictait leur cons… Rejoindre Lénine au pays de l'espoir bolchévique pour b… nouveau monde.
...Ich bin Ewig...
UN ANGE DANS LE CIEL DE PETROGRAD
Dès le lendemain de la prise du palais d'Hiver, l'aviatrice célèbre Farouge survolait le ciel de Petrograd, lançant des tracts de victoire. On la voit ici, survolant la forteresse Pierre et Paul. (Photo Frank Stern)

And it's not by chance that I recognize the couple in the crowd following the capture of the Winter Palace, or in Moscow along with Kamenev and Trotsky. Frank is the Party's official photographer. And Farouge, "the Red angel," is in every photo. The couple as one, on page one, that is...

But the Communist idyll is short-lived. Lenin has little taste for the spiritual allusions of the XXe Ciel. His revolution is an earthly one and the work of educating the masses cannot be encumbered with ambiguities, suspect of "petty bourgeois, counter-revolutionary elitism." Frank's coverage of the depredations of the Winter Palace by the Red guards and the pillaging of Orthodox churches lead to the photographer's disgrace and the banning of the paper.

The end of 1918, the Party's official paper reads that Comrade Frank Stern has been named director of propaganda in the Carpathian Mountains. As such, he's assisting the mission of the American journalist John Reed, crisscrossing the snow-covered lands on board those legendary propaganda trains. The article is published between the obituaries and a story about some dogs that had been run over.

The last photo of the couple in Russia shows them at the train platform before his departure for the Carpathians on board the Red Star. Farouge is not going along. Frank alone still looks toward the sky. Utopia is separating them.

At the end of 1920, the XXe Ciel experiences its first eclipse.

November 31, 1924. It's a mild fall. At day's end, I'm relaxing along the central walkway of the winter garden.

At 3:31, I hear the cawing of a crow. And I recognize the bird.

He doesn't bring me the latest issue of XXe Ciel, but of Pravda.

The first page celebrates Comrade Stalin and the tenth anniversary of the October Revolution. For the occasion, the paper republishes the eternal icon of the first leader of the Communist party haranguing the Muscovite crowd from atop his podium. Eternal, aside from several details...

...Kamenev, Trotsky, and Farouge have disappeared from the dais. AndFrank, too. The photo has been doctored and rewrites History. All of the first communists have been excluded from the Party, all censored. Frank is censored.

A cruel irony, in the anniversary column, I learn officially some eight years later that the propaganda train the Red Star was blown up in the Carpathians, shelled by the counter-revolutionary White armies. A valiant comrade photographer, a comrade of Lenin from the very beginning, died heroically along with all his heroic comrades. No survivors. From then on, Frank became for me like the angel of his photographs: even if I never see him, he's ever present.

Click. London, September 31, 1932. The years have passed. I travel a lot.
During an air show, I cross paths with Fabienne Rouge-Dyeu. She's performing.

John, my companion, would be flattered to meet the star. I propose to introduce the two of them.

Despite the number of years gone by, she seems to recognize me. She's as cheerful as ever. I politely congratulate her for her exploits.

At her side, a young boy observes me. Her son, seemingly.

Evening Argus

SUSSEX DAILY NEWS

Monday May 18, 1934

FAROUGE, FIRST WOMAN OVER THE TOP OF THE WORLD

Conquest of Everest

TWO STABBED IN

SUR PETROGRA

AVIATION

Le Monde

15, rue Falguière, 75501 Paris Cedex 15

Après Yeager, Fabienne Rouge-Dyeu passe le mur du son sur un Leduc 0.10

Impossible n'est pas français

10

F. ANGE

Over some 20 years, I continue to follow the evolution of the aviatrix's brilliant career via newspaper headlines... From time to time, I stumble on a photo that leaves me troubled...

...But each time, I recall our last meeting in London and I tell myself that photos lie... That time, I saw right away that Fabienne had aged...

...Eva? Are you awake?

...Lucienne...You got any more Saint Michael cigarettes?

You know the nurse took them away from me!...
That beats all! usually people condemned to death have a right to a cigarette, don't they?!!
You're not gonna get started again, are you?

Oh yes! She'll see us all in the grave before she'll stop giving us hell!!

Gabriel Davis!! The last time we met was in California and you were claiming to have the secret of life eternal!!...
As you can see, it was the boasting of an ambitious, young physician...I've gotten a bit older, haven't I?

Don't be so modest! All surgeons are convinced they hold the power of life and death over their patients. All the more so with a biologist specializing in genetic cloning...
...and all psychoanalysts are crazy enough to believe they can transform this life!

Hmm! You look fine, Eva. Tell me why they admitted you to this hospital... Are you that angry with them?

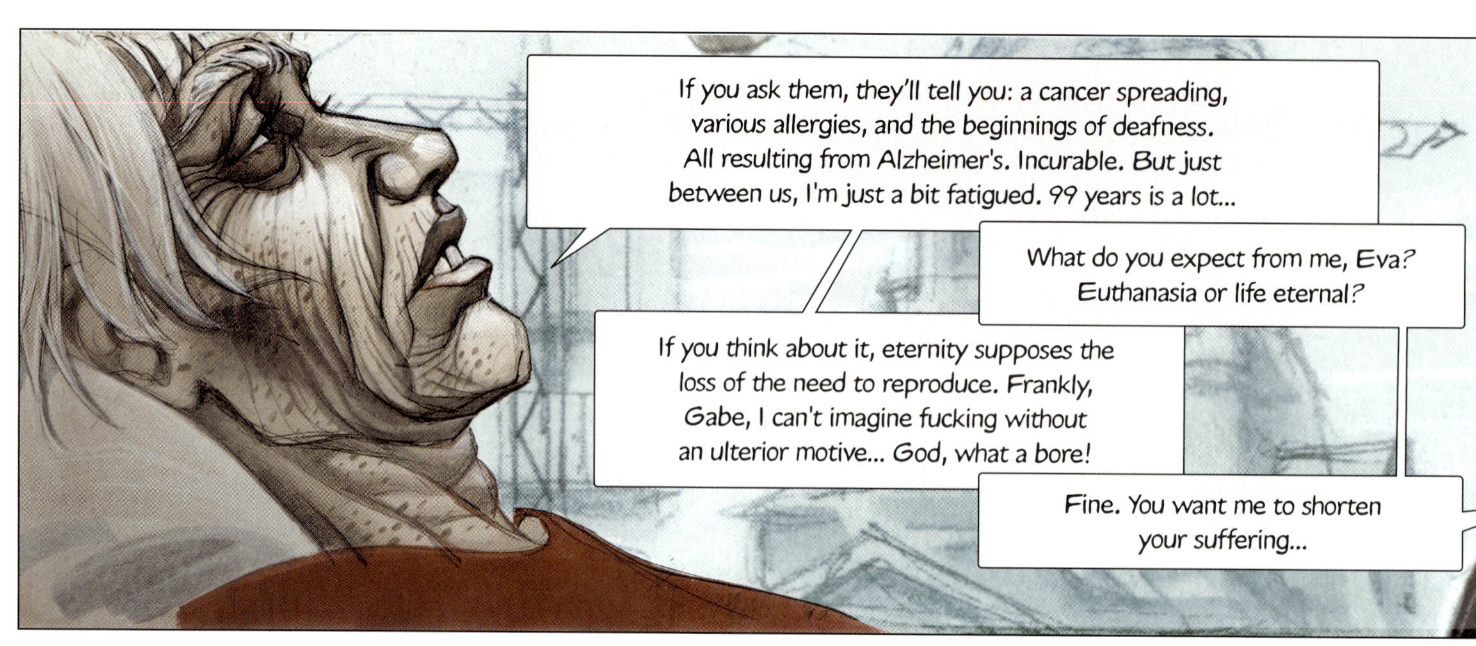
If you ask them, they'll tell you: a cancer spreading, various allergies, and the beginnings of deafness. All resulting from Alzheimer's. Incurable. But just between us, I'm just a bit fatigued. 99 years is a lot...
What do you expect from me, Eva? Euthanasia or life eternal?
If you think about it, eternity supposes the loss of the need to reproduce. Frankly, Gabe, I can't imagine fucking without an ulterior motive... God, what a bore!
Fine. You want me to shorten your suffering...

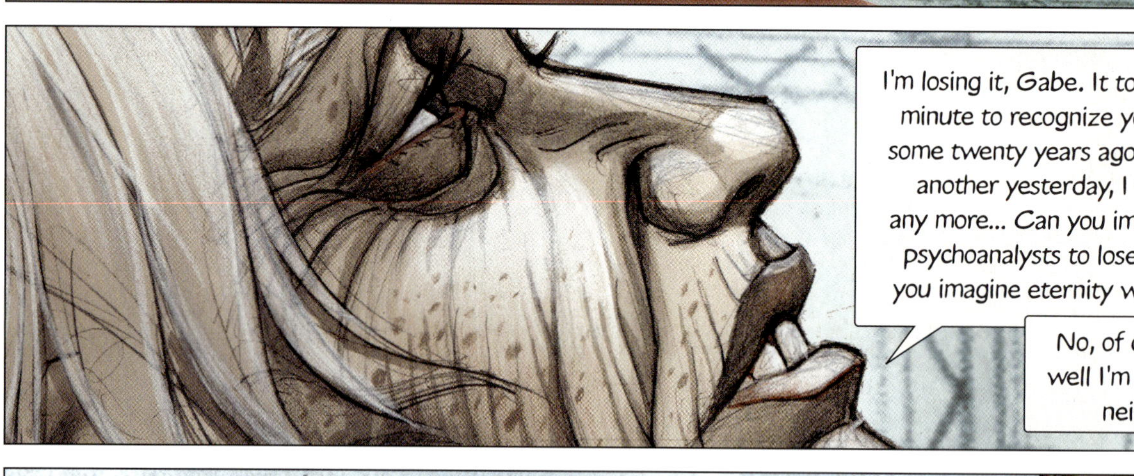
I'm losing it, Gabe. It took me more than half a minute to recognize you. Granted that was some twenty years ago. But if we'd seen one another yesterday, I wouldn't remember any more... Can you imagine what it's like for psychoanalysts to lose their memory? Can you imagine eternity without remembering?
No, of course not! You know very well I'm nothing but a butcher with neither a brain nor soul...

...But, on the contrary, one with professional ethics...Sorry, Eva, I'm against euthanasia.

No joke! You've got principles now? ...And your research on rejuvenating cells, your genetic experiments on Frank Stern, that was ethics?
I don't know what you're talking about.

Listen Gabe, I don't give a damn if I die fast or not. But before that, I want to understand. I've been part of this profession my whole life in order to understand. So, spit it out... You operated on Frank after his suicide. How old was he in 1973?

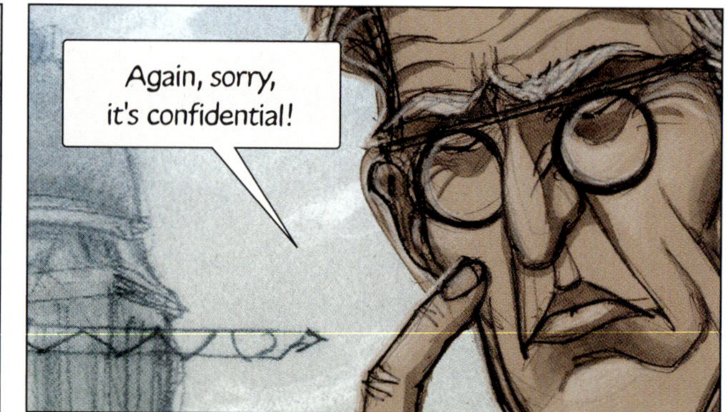
Again, sorry, it's confidential!

..Otherwise, what can I do for you since I cannot save you?
Give me a cigarette.

You know very well that it's bad for your lungs.

THEN GET THE HELL OUT, YOU QUEER!!

...WAIT! Don't leave so quick!
I don't know what that old crone means to you, young lady, but I wish you lots of courage! ...This whole voyage from London to hear her say that to me!!!

I'm the only one at fault! Eva never asked for anyone's help! I'm the one who took the initiative to call you.

...because now the only thing that can help her live is this!!

Better still! All this for a photo!? Are you really trying to make me lose my composure, young lady??

...Please, look ...Isn't that you in the picture there, along with Nathan Uriel and Raphael Von Wergifüss? And beside you, Eva claims that could be my mother. Did you know her?...

...Woodstock, '69 ...Hmm, why yes! That was me... but your Vietnamese woman there, on the contrary, I barely knew her. All I know is that several years later she leapt from the Golden Gate Bridge to meet God. Splash! Overdose!

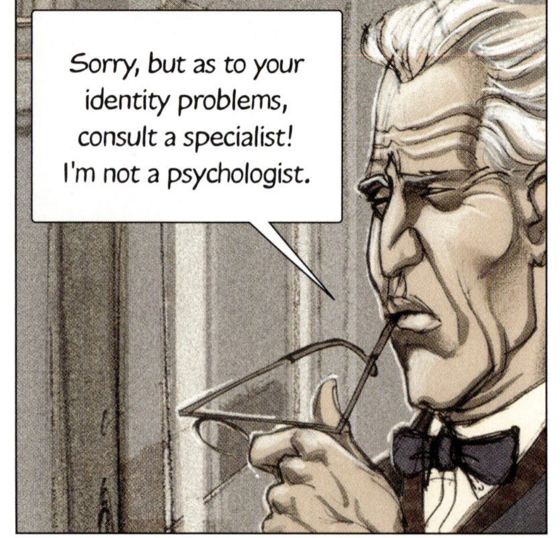
Sorry, but as to your identity problems, consult a specialist! I'm not a psychologist.

...But there in the foreground, isn't that Eva's brother?
No. He wasn't with us at Woodstock.

Look at the blur...Clearly this person was added in later, during its development...

...the photo is doctored, young lady. Moreover, I'll repeat to you, I've never met Frank Stern...
You hadn't told me so!

Come now, dear... It's not my place to tell you that, but... Frank has never been but fantasy in his sister's mind, it's obvious... She think he's eternal...
That a sister takes her adored brother for a figurative angel is normal. But to do so literally falls under the heading of psychiatry.

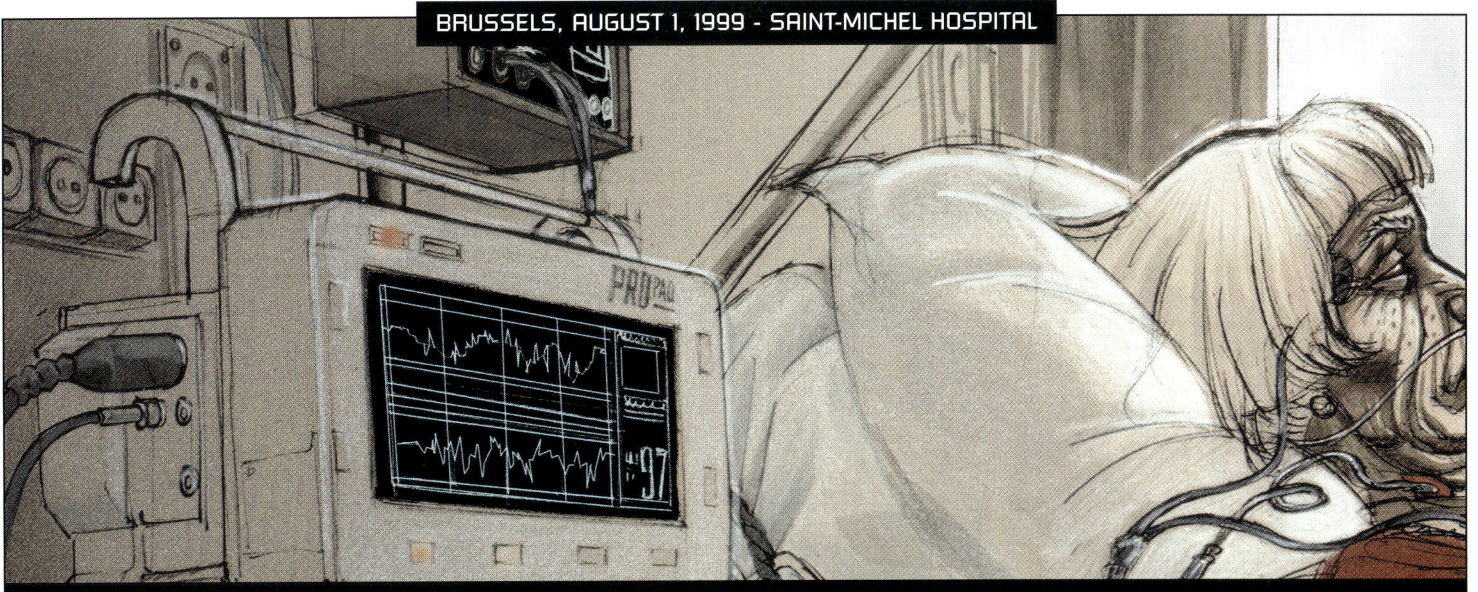

It was a painful night. But when I awake, Lucienne is there... With a message from @nonymous and a gift...

At a bookseller's she found a rare copy of the XXè Ciel that I'd have preferred to have never seen published. It dates from November 1942. Back then, it circulated inside the jackets of resistors. So that everyone would know the truth... Her joy and pride are such that I don't breathe a word to her of my sleeplessness...

...Nor of my emotion. She didn't experience the rise of the Nazis during the '30s. She doesn't know...

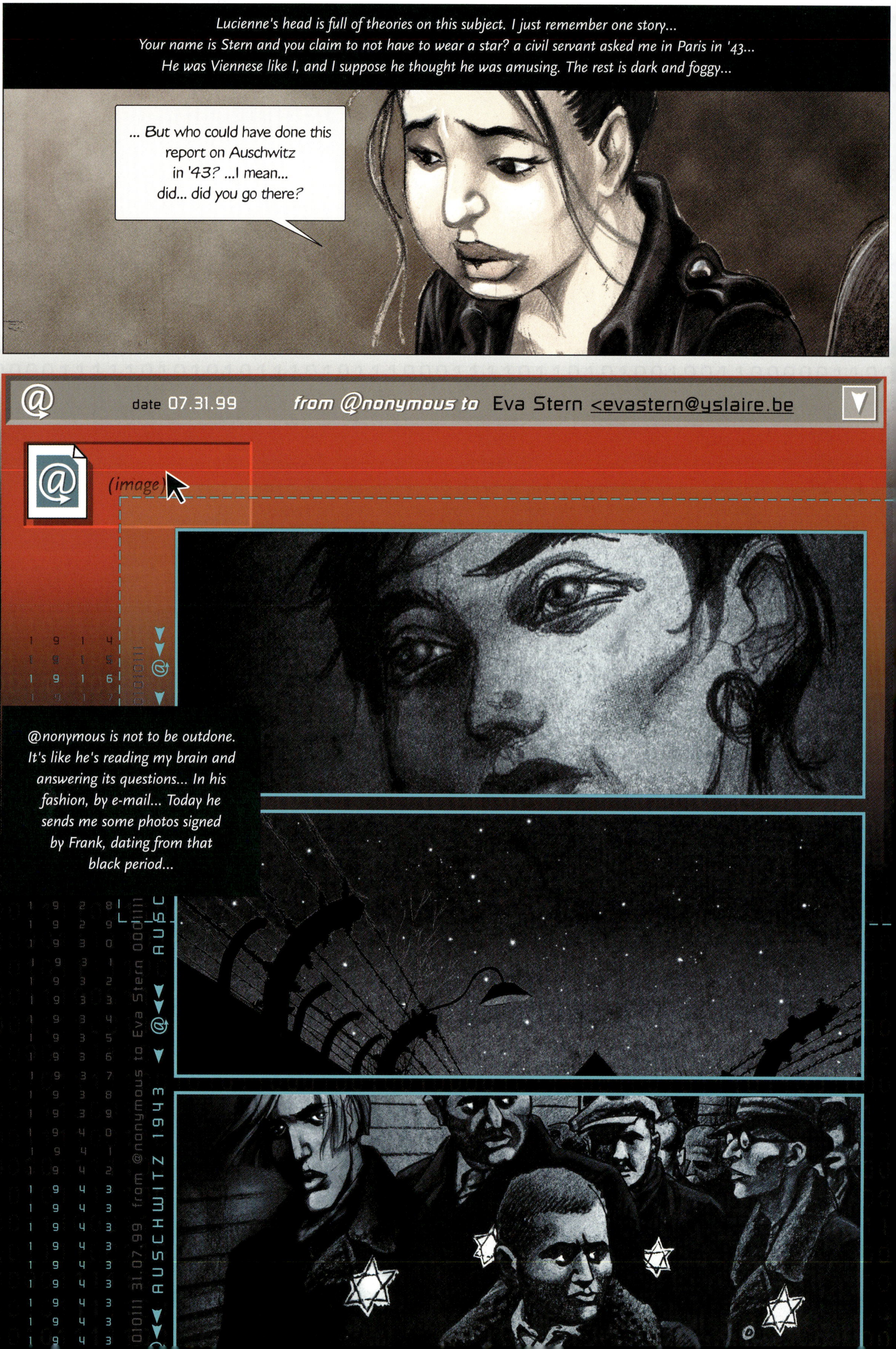

Lucienne's head is full of theories on this subject. I just remember one story...
Your name is Stern and you claim to not have to wear a star? a civil servant asked me in Paris in '43...
He was Viennese like I, and I suppose he thought he was amusing. The rest is dark and foggy...

... But who could have done this report on Auschwitz in '43? ...I mean... did... did you go there?
date 07.31.99 from @nonymous to Eva Stern <evastern@yslaire.be
(image)

@nonymous is not to be outdone. It's like he's reading my brain and answering its questions... In his fashion, by e-mail... Today he sends me some photos signed by Frank, dating from that black period...

31.07.99 from @nonymous to Eva Stern

AUSCHWITZ 1943

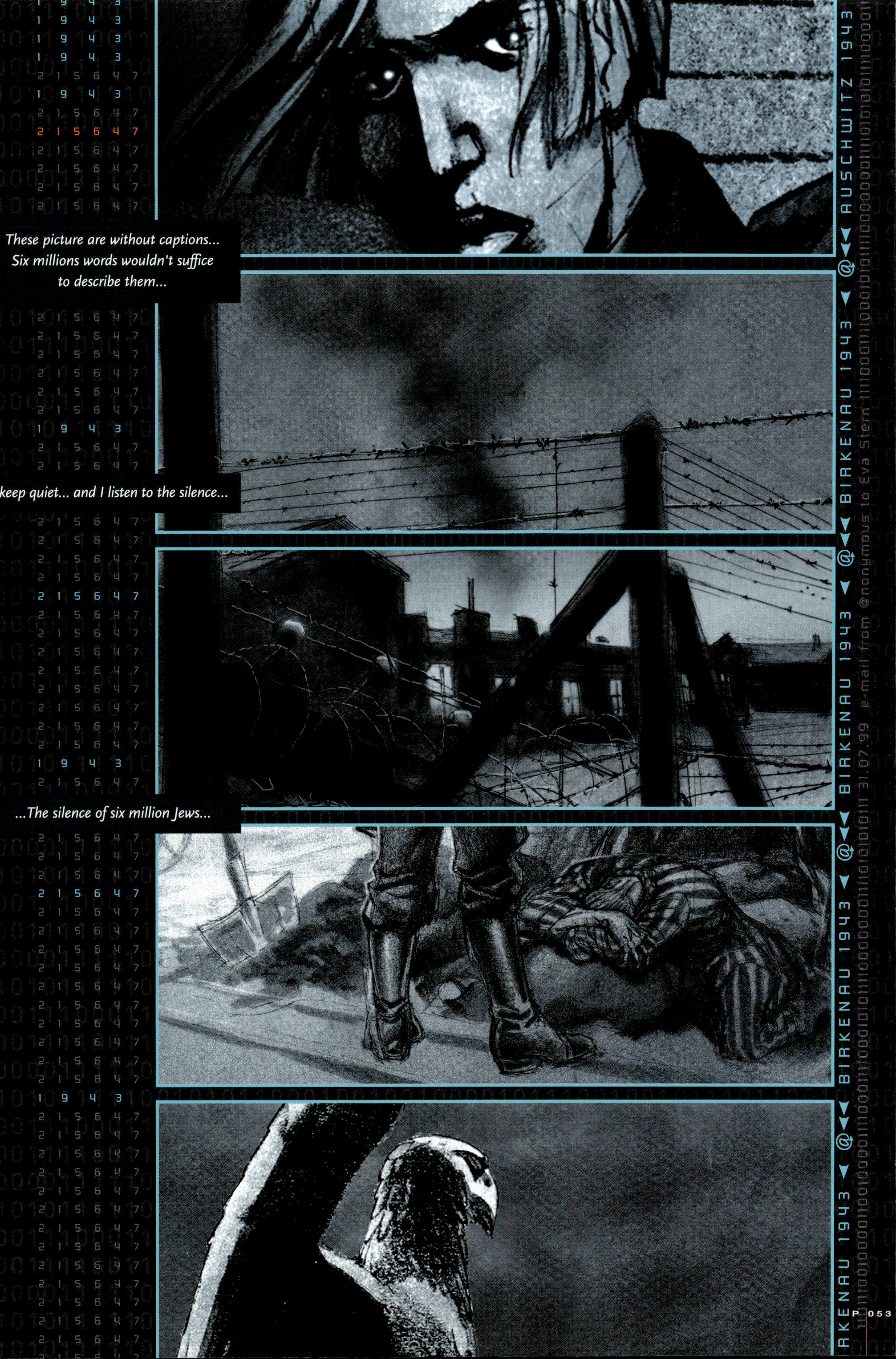

These picture are without captions...
Six millions words wouldn't suffice
to describe them...

keep quiet... and I listen to the silence...

...The silence of six million Jews...

e-mail from @nonymous to Eva Stern 31.07.99

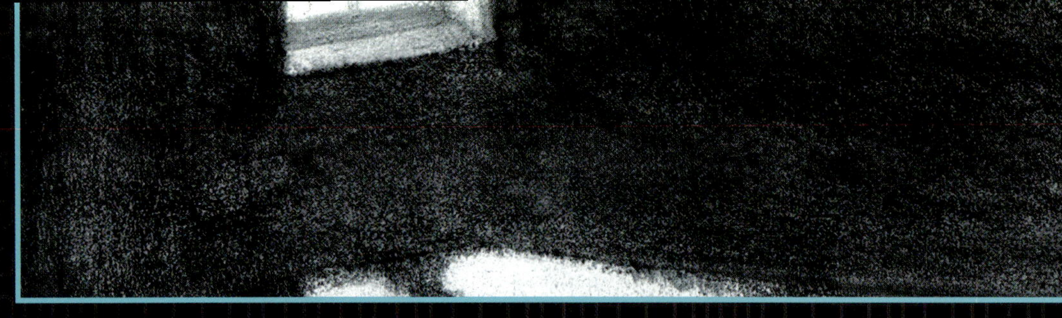

e-mail from @nonymous to Eva Stern 31.07.99

AUSCHWITZ 1944

VARSOVIE 1944 @ VARSOVIE 1944 @ VARSOVIE 1944 @ VARSOVIE 1944 VARSOVIE 1944 @ AUSCHWITZ 194
31.07.99 e-mail from @nonymous to Eva Stern
1944
215647
6000000
P 05

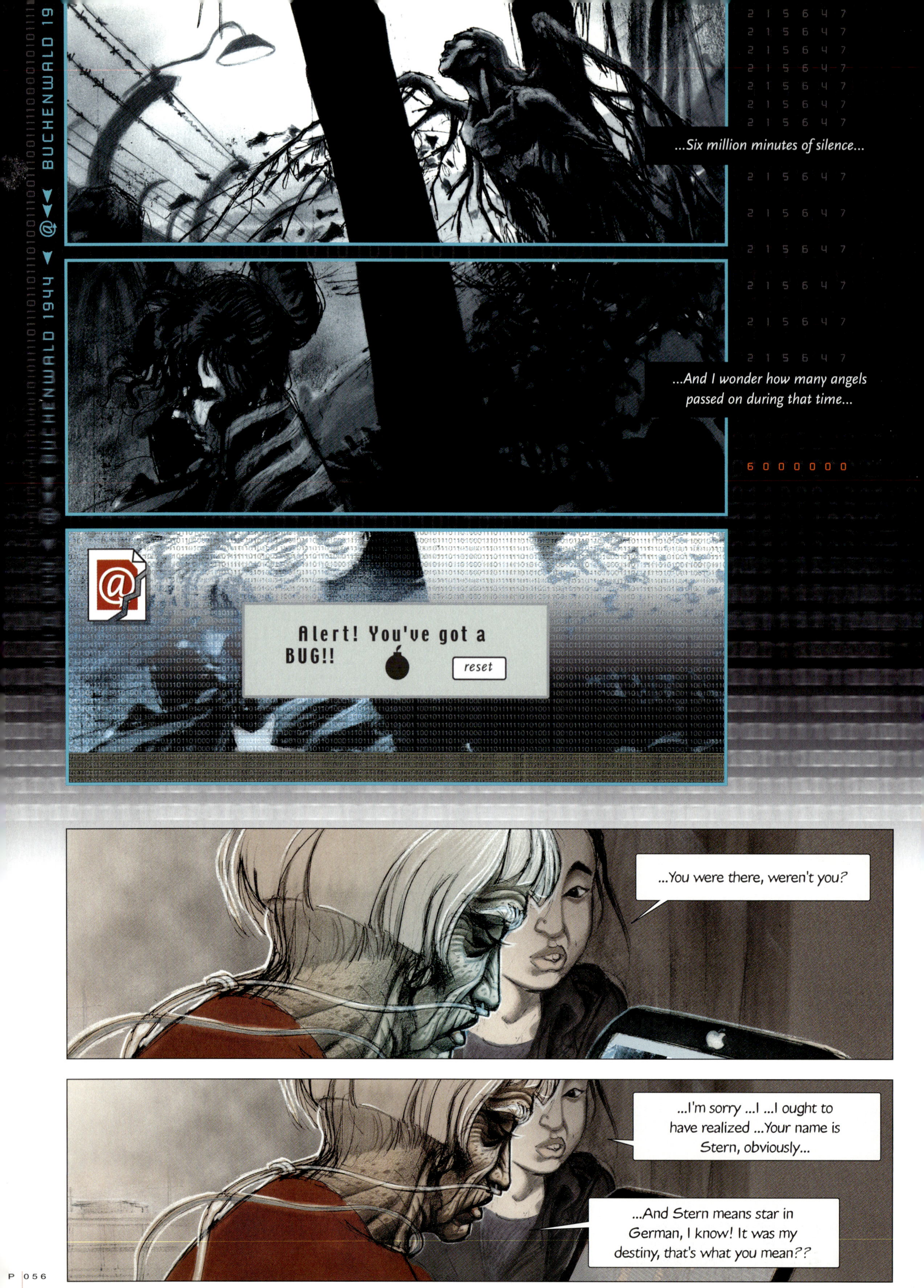

BUCHENWALD 1944 ◄ @ ◄◄ BUCHENWALD 19

...Six million minutes of silence...

...And I wonder how many angels passed on during that time...

6 0 0 0 0 0 0

Alert! You've got a BUG!!

reset

...You were there, weren't you?

...I'm sorry ...I ...I ought to have realized ...Your name is Stern, obviously...
...And Stern means star in German, I know! It was my destiny, that's what you mean??

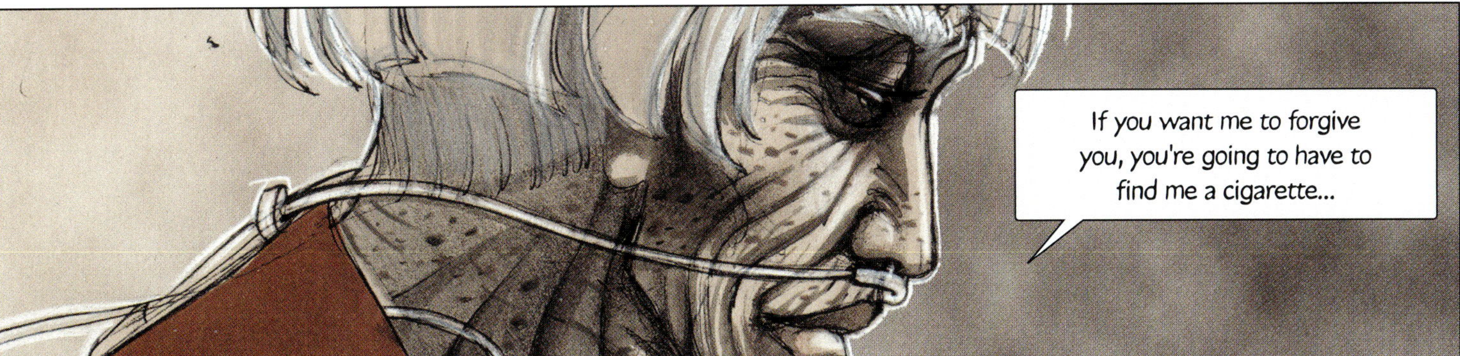

If you want me to forgive you, you're going to have to find me a cigarette...

And did Gabriel also tell you that I underwent several stays in a psychiatric hospital?
No, no... well... he implied it...

...That I was always something of a pathological liar... ?

You can leave now. The crazy, old woman has no more stories to tell.

Poor Lucienne, she won't finish her paper with me. Those must be the last words I say to her.
The following months, she still comes to see me twice or three times, and @nonymous passes on...

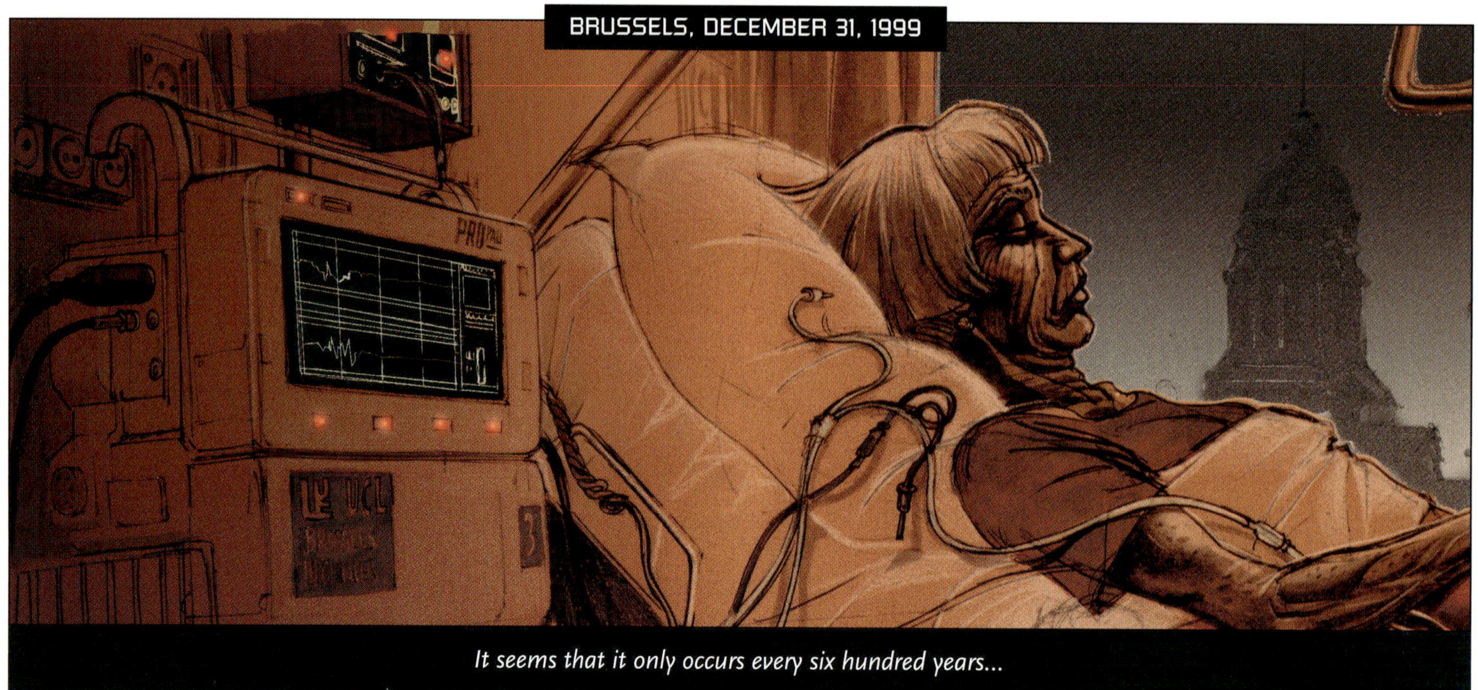
BRUSSELS, DECEMBER 31, 1999
It seems that it only occurs every six hundred years...

...The moon eclipsing the sun. I remember. It was on August 13, 1999. There were millions of people in the world looking at the sky for the space of a few seconds. It's rare for millions of people to look at the sky together at the same time... religiously... (With darkened glasses, all the same. To not let themselves be dazzled by the supernatural...)

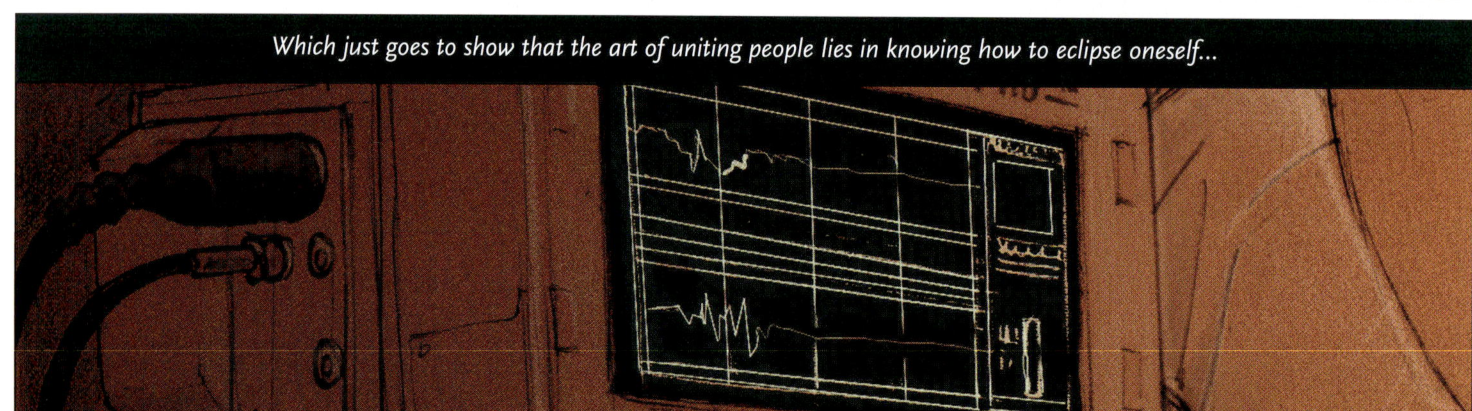
Which just goes to show that the art of uniting people lies in knowing how to eclipse oneself...

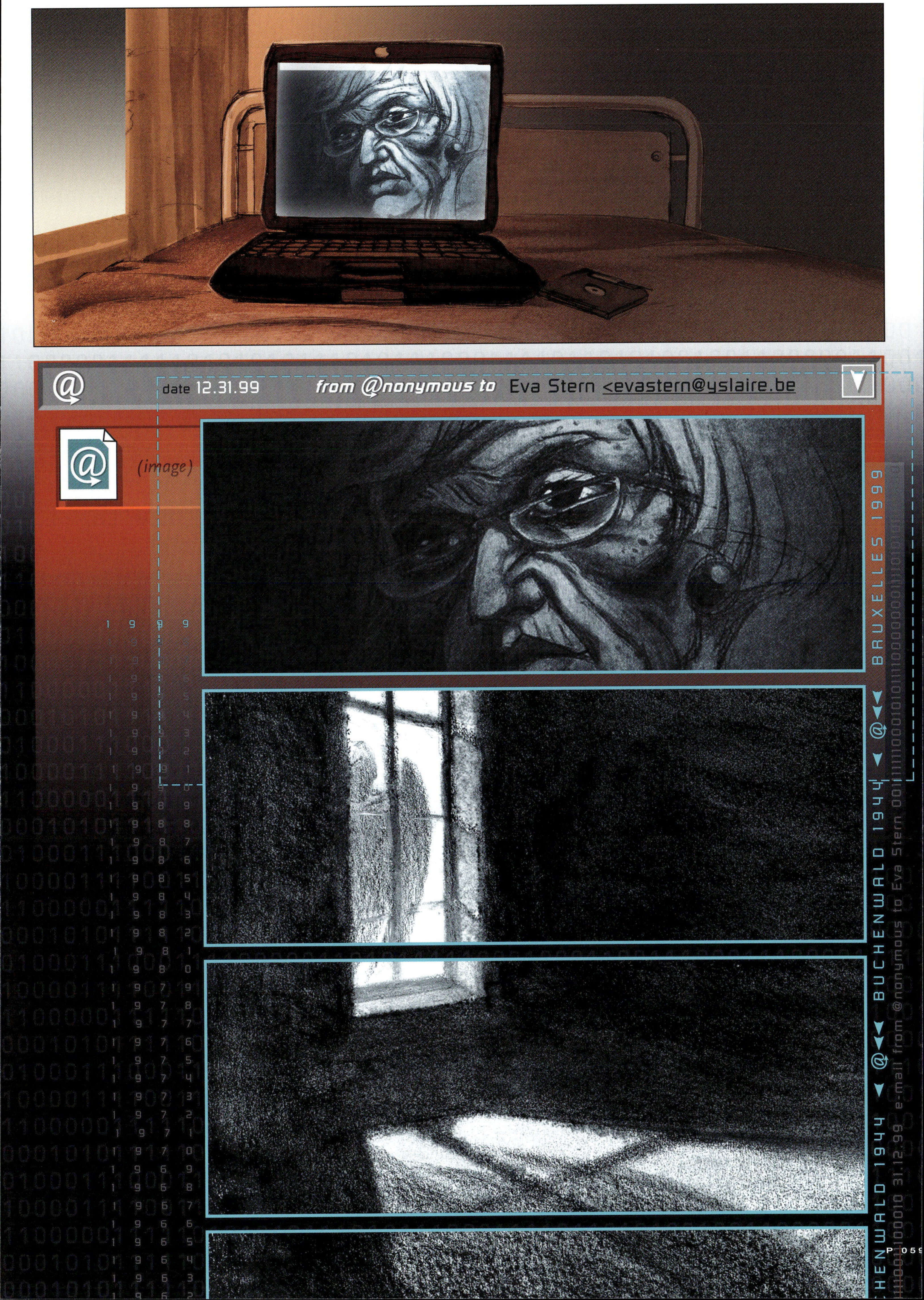

date 12.31.99 *from @nonymous to* Eva Stern <evastern@yslaire.be

(image)

BUCHENWALD 1944 ◄ @◄◄ BUCHENWALD 1944 ◄ @◄◄ BRUXELLES 1999

e-mail from @nonymous to Eva Stern 31.12.99

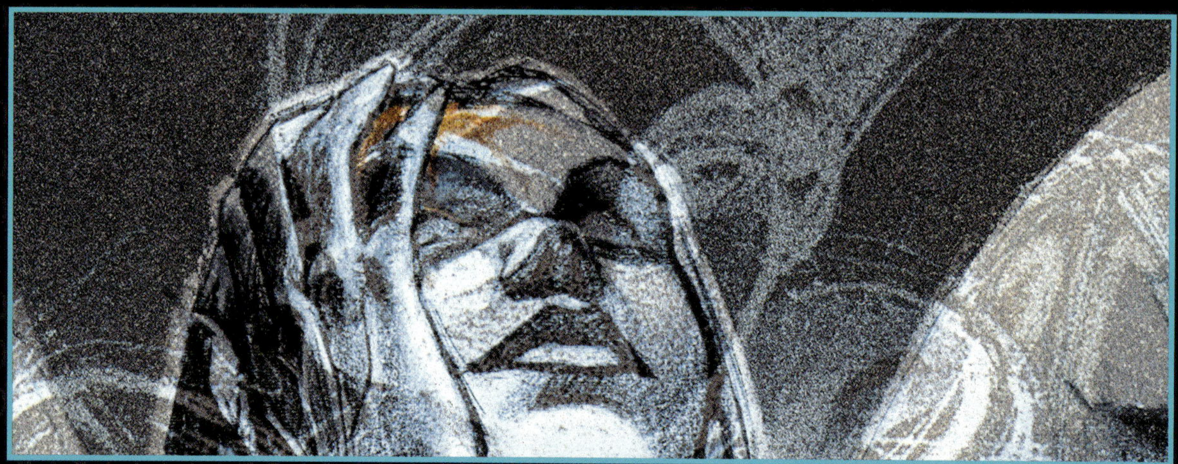

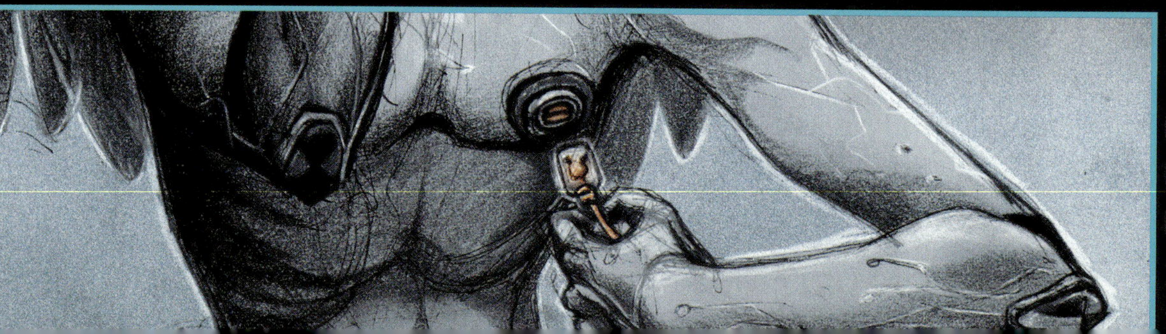

Alert! You've got a BUG!!
reset

Alert! You've got a BUG!!

reset

Alert! You've got a BUG!!

reset

Alert! You've got a BUG!!

reset

reset

THE NIKOPOL TRILOGY
By Enki Bilal

Hardcover album, Full color, 176 pages. $39,95

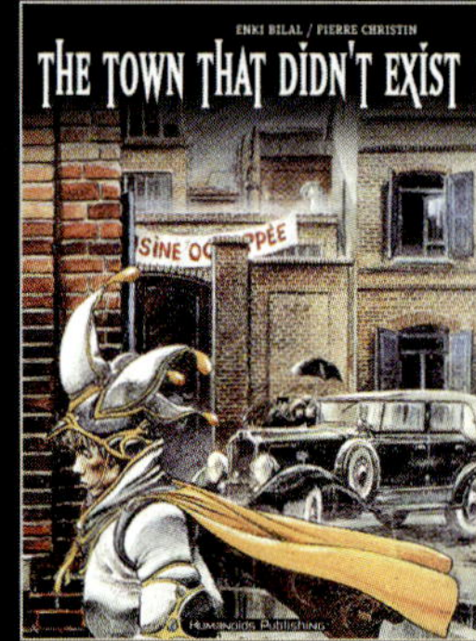

THE TOWN THAT DIDN'T EXIST
By Enki Bilal

Hardcover album, Full color, 56 pages. $14,95

THE TECHNOPRIESTS
VOL.1
VOL.2
VOL.3
By Alexandro Jodorowsky, Zoran Janjetov & Fred Beltran

Hardcover album, Full color, 56 pages. $14,95

THE FOURTH POWER
By Juan Gimenez

Hardcover album, Full color, 64 pages. $14,95

LEO ROA
VOL.1
THE TRUE TALE OF LEO ROA
VOL.2
AN ODYSSEY BACK IN TIME
By Juan Gimenez

Hardcover album, Full color, 60 pages. $14,95

THE DORMANT BEAST
By Enki Bilal

Paperback graphic novel, 72 pages. $10,95

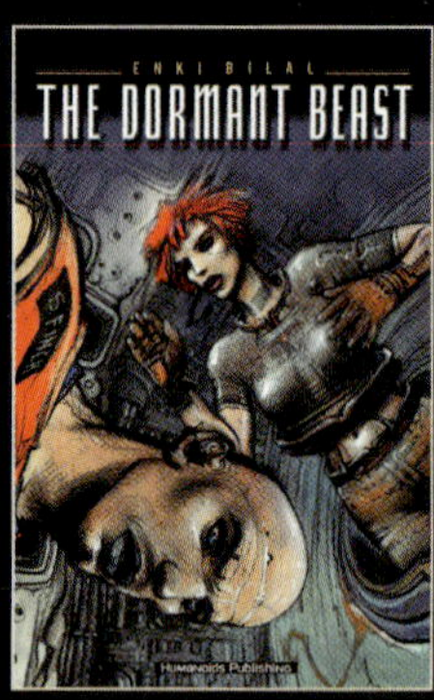

FOM CLOUD 99, MEMORIES PART 1
By Yslaire

Hardcover album, Full color, 64 pages. $14,95

THE WHITE LAMA
VOL.1
VOL.2
VOL.3
VOL.4
VOL.5
VOL.6
By Georges Bess & Alexandro Jodorowsky

Hardcover album, Full color, 48 pages. $14,95

THE BOK OF JACK
By Olivier Boiscommun & Denis Pierre Filippi

Hardcover album, Full color, 48 pages. $14,95

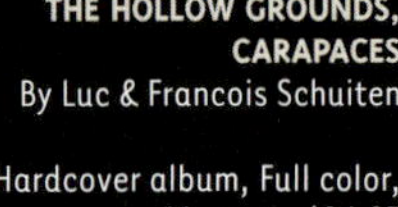

THE HOLLOW GROUNDS, CARAPACES
By Luc & Francois Schuiten

Hardcover album, Full color, 64 pages. $14,95

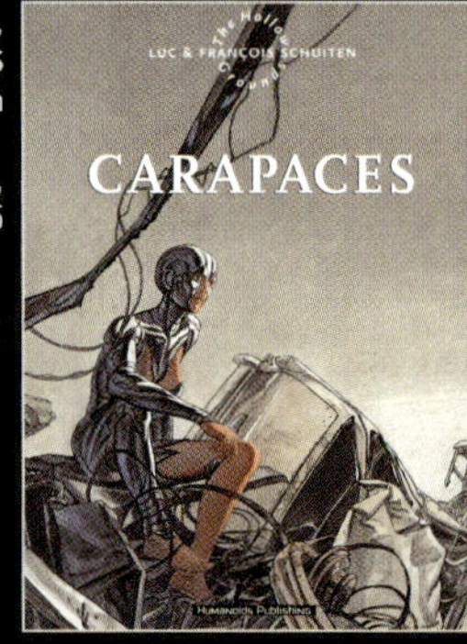

THE HOLLOW GROUNDS, ZARA
By Luc & Francois Schuiten

Hardcover album, Full color, 58 pages. $14,95

THE HOLLOW GROUNDS, NOGEGON
By Luc & Francois Schuiten

Hardcover album, Full color, 72 pages. $14,95

Available at comic book retailers, your neighborhood book store and quality websites.

Humanoids Publishing™

PO Box 931658, Hollywood, CA 90093 Fax (323) 850-5804 cs@humanoids-publishing.com
www.metabarons.com • www.humanoids-publishing.com

Photographic Credits:

«Concentration camps, Auschwitz, Poland», Raymond Depardon, Magnum Photos.
«Foetus», Lennart Nilson, Life Magazine, DR

Page 15 modified for release in the United States due to explicit sexual content.

Phsychoanalytic Consultant: Laurence Erlich

Graphic Design Concept and Execution : Yslaire and D. Gonord

US Edition Graphic Design and Adaptation : Thierry Frissen

US Edition Computer Lettering : Jens Kristen

Editorial Consultant : Sébastien Gnaedig

Accomplice: Eric Verhoest

From Cloud 99 - Memories part 2
Translation by Dr. Joe Johnson

Printed in Belgium. Bound in France.
Humanoids Publishing and the Humanoids Publishing Logo are trademarks of Les Humanoides Associes S. A. Geneva (Switzerland) registered in various categories and countries.
Humanoids Publishing, a division of Humanoids Group.

ISBN : 1-930652-01-1

Alert! You've got a BUG!!
reset
LE XX
JOURNAL DES AMES
Ich bi
Rédacteur en chef: Werner Yeler
LE XXe CIEL
1re Année - N° 2
31 OCTOBRE 1916
JOURNAL DES AMES
Dyeu est-il mo
FORMIDABLE
AVEC FURIE